# Firecracker

## Claire's Journey

## Mia Fliers

For
Suzan, who began the whole thing
&
Jen, who got me to the end

# PROLOGUE

Frank, her bodyguard, was close now, right behind her. Claire quickened her steps, anxious to get this whole experience behind her. She hadn't anticipated needing a bodyguard; it seemed excessive. As they crossed the plaza, she noted that Frank had moved up beside her, shielding her from the street, she guessed.

*Why must I do this; how did they talk me into this?* she thought. Breath coming more quickly now. Her heels were higher than she usually tolerated. The stockings were so annoying on such a hot day.

Shots rang out—*pop, pop.*

Frank grabbed her arm, pulling her to him, forcing her to run. The plaza stretched out ahead of them—so far to the tall glass doors. Where were the shots coming from? What were they shooting at?

Suddenly Frank's grip was gone; he fell to the pavement, causing her to stumble. He yelled at her, "*RUN!*"

Another shot.

Claire couldn't stop. She was back on her feet. She ran as best she could in the tight skirt and high heels. She staggered at last into the heavy glass door, pushing it away from her, hoping it was bulletproofed. Where could she hide?

*Pop. Pop.* This time hitting the glass doors. They held.

*They are after me!* Her mind screamed: *Got to find a way out!*

Crowds of workers and visitors poured into the lobby of the building. She removed her navy blue jacket as she moved toward them, hoping her pale blue silk blouse would make her less recognizable in the crowd.

She edged her way around people, toward the elevator.

A man stood still in front of her escape route—looking for her? *Can't take a chance,* she whispered to herself. *Where? A sign to the cafeteria!* Maybe a back door to a loading dock.

She walked quickly, unnoticed in the milling crowd, moving—and there was the door. She eased through, running through the kitchen, then out the door that led to an alley.

*Which way to turn? The park.* She rushed toward the long driveway leading away from the building. She had to get away.

# CHAPTER 1

Could it have been three years ago? Her first encounter with Casey Malone? Shocked had been her initial reaction.

Claire was hostessing in a high-end restaurant in uptown when suddenly, a stocky, well-muscled man approached her. But instead of taking the menu offered, Casey's man made it clear that she was to come with him. She stepped back and turned away to summon the owner, Bruno. The man took her elbow and marched her through the front entrance, passing gawking patrons waiting in line to be seated. She went, too stunned to utter a sound as the man pulled her toward the waiting limousine.

"What are you doing?" she finally blurted.

Without comment, he pushed Claire

unceremoniously into the waiting vehicle, which immediately took off.

Shaken and stunned at what had just happened, she blanched as she looked at the man sitting across from her. She tried not to stare at his scar, which started at his temple and ran down his face, making his lip curl slightly. He was not exactly old, but that didn't make him any less menacing.

He gazed at her intently but said nothing for a full minute. "So, you are Claire."

She was still too shocked to say anything. *Who is this guy? How does he know me?*

"You don't have to be scared. I just needed to meet you before hiring you for the project I have in mind."

"*Hire* me?" she sputtered.

"My contacts told me you are perfect for what I need: you're attractive, not too flashy, classy looking, bright—can talk to the kind of people I need to persuade."

Her voice shrill with her growing apprehension, she asked, "What are you talking about? Why am I here?"

"I wanted to see for myself," he replied. "But you need to smarten up the wardrobe more—you know

—classy, expensive. Maggie will get you to the right people. Not so much makeup, the hair—all that stuff. Then we'll see."

"See what?"

Casey smirked. "Whether you're worth a hundred grand a year plus an expense account—to start." He waited for her reaction. Somewhat disappointed at her lack of enthusiasm, he more sternly announced, "However, everything you see, learn, hear about me, or my business is strictly between you and me. No exceptions." Casey sat back, obviously pleased with how he was handling this meeting.

"Why would I want to know anything about you or your business? I don't even know your name!"

"Casey Malone. Of course, you heard of me?"

She took a deep breath. "Maybe. No. Yes. I don't know." Claire's initial fear gave way to intense curiosity. Of course, she had heard of Casey Malone: billionaire, up from the streets the hard way; mixed reviews on his businesses, real estate, she thought. Legit? Or not so much? Who knew?

*But why her? That kind of money! Why not her?* However, the real question was, what did he want from her? Questions were flying rapidly through her mind.

"I need you to be my face, my front."

She quickly looked away from his scarred face.

"Maggie will give you all the particulars. Thank you for coming, Claire."

The limo had pulled over in front of her apartment.

"Why am I *here*? I have to go back to work," she declared.

His driver was already opening her door.

Nervously she asked, "How do you know where I live?"

No answer.

As she got out, she began asking again, but Casey stopped her. "Maggie will help you find a more appropriate apartment."

She stood aghast, looking at him as his window closed, and the limo roared off.

*Who in the hell was Maggie?*

# CHAPTER 2

Before meeting Claire, Casey wanted the full scoop on her.

He called Maggie into his office. She entered with a spring in her step.

"You're lookin' good this morning, Maggie," he said as he took in her trim 5'2" figure.

They had known each other since grade school. Always sassy, with bright red ribbons in her dark brown hair. She was the one person in his life he trusted implicitly.

"Nothing like a spa day," Maggie said.

Casey uttered his usual "huh," and picked up a dossier from his desk. "We've work to do."

She smiled and made her way to the coffee hutch in the far corner. She poured a cup for herself and one for Casey, with his usual 4 lumps of sugar and heavy cream. After she handed him his cup, she settled herself in front of his desk, crossing her legs for his benefit, pen and pad out and ready.

"I want you to investigate what Claire is up to. She's finished school, and I want to know what she is doing. And Maggie, I want your opinion—is she ready to bring into the fold? Can she fit in?"

Maggie looked up and inched forward in her chair. "Are you sure that's a good idea, Casey? We don't really know her—or how she may view—the projects, you know."

"That's what I want you to take a gander at. Look, there is no one else to take care of her. If she fits in—great! That would be the easiest. If not—well, I've done my best."

Maggie looked at him, a bit puzzled. This didn't feel right. If anyone gave them trouble, she always knew Casey would look out for them.

"You're sure, Casey?"

One look from him made it clear.

"I'll get on it right away. Anything else?"

"No, just get it moving."

Maggie was bothered, but she had her marching orders, and that was that. OK, first things first: she sat at her desk and punched the extension that connected her with two watchers she trusted. She described the assignment, making it clear that ASAP meant more than fast.

All these years she had handled the anonymous checks to the private schools that Claire attended, or got rid of the minor scrapes the girl had gotten herself into. She understood that he was honoring his promise to Claire's mother. But bringing her on board? And what if she didn't fit? The way he seemed so coldly to dismiss the issue bothered her. No, this didn't feel good to her at all.

Maggie had relied on Casey ever since her best friend, Ruthie, Claire's mother, was killed. It had finally dawned on her that Casey had become a force to be reckoned with, and he was the one person who could and would protect her.

As a kid, she'd had a silly crush on him, but he never let her get that close until he offered her a job in his growing company—as his personal assistant. She couldn't even type! But he sent her to school at night to get the skills he needed her to have. It thrilled her to discover that she excelled.

She was totally devoted to Casey Malone. No one else had ever protected her or helped her in any way. No matter what—Casey was her hero. She assured herself that it would all work out.

It didn't take long for Maggie to bring Casey the information he'd ordered. He was convinced Claire was who he wanted in his growing organization. He instructed Maggie that they were to hire her immediately.

\* \* \*

Claire gave two weeks' notice to Bruno, her boss at the restaurant, and then warned Lucky, her roommate and friend, that she was moving out. And Claire went to work for Casey Malone!

She still didn't know how to feel about this sudden change in her life. The first week was full of whirlwind activity: her spacious new apartment, then shadowing Maggie through her days. Little by little, she was becoming acquainted with the diverse aspects of his enterprise.

She met clients or potential buyers, got indoctrinated into the computer system and its many security features, and started to get used to having an office all to herself. It was exciting but overwhelming.

At week's end, Maggie let her know it was time to go shopping.

"Per Casey's instructions; No arguments!"

As uneasy as Claire felt about accepting such generosity, Maggie made it clear that if she wanted to work for him, she was to accept graciously.

\* \* \*

Casey took a sip of his coffee as he sat back in his chair. Maggie had finished reporting on her progress with Claire. He liked watching Maggie as she left and closed the door behind her.

He got it. He could tell that Maggie was still uneasy at how fast everything was progressing.

Casey reviewed his first personal interaction with Claire. He had promised her mother, Ruthie, that he would protect her—and that included from him. But if he was ever going to bring her into the organization, it had to happen now.

Happily, she was measuring up to his expectations. She could be used to great advantage. He needed her look and the education he had provided her with anonymous scholarships and grants. Her lack of fear intrigued him. Yes, she would do. Maggie would take care of the rest.

Enjoying his coffee as he took in his spectacular view of the City, he thought about those two: Maggie and her best friend, Ruthie. He never forgot that night he'd been jumped on his way home. Stupidly, he and his buddy, Sam, had taken a shortcut right through Little Italy. He got away after a fierce fight that left a scar down the left side of his face. He was lucky that Sam had been with him. The knife had barely missed his eye. When the hoodlums took off, Sam, with great bravado, assured Casey that he could always depend on him to have his back. *Yeah, look at how that turned out.*

Casey sighed. *Sam. Why did he have to become such an SOB?*

When he got to his own block, there on the stoop of their brownstone were Ruthie and Maggie, playing their stupid game of jacks. He started running toward them, yelling, "What's the matter with you two? Ruthie, get upstairs; no, no argument. How many times do you have to be warned to be inside when it's dark? That street light could be shot out in a second."

The girls were shocked at the blood on his face,

and they scrambled to obey his commands.

"Come on, Maggie," he said, "I'll walk you home."

Maggie tried to protest; she only lived two buildings down the block.

He stopped her, and more calmly explained, "I promised Uncle Donnie before he went to prison that I would take care of you and Ruthie. That I would protect you. And I keep my promises. So just shut up and start walking."

Casey chuckled to himself as he remembered how angry he had been. Those girls just never listened to him!

He grimaced. Well, years later, that finally changed. Ruthie was fatally hit by a bullet when bringing five-year-old Claire home from the park. *Had Sam been with those gangsters?* He thought so, but he never knew for sure.

Maggie turned to him for protection and later, even guidance. Eventually, he took her under his wing and brought her into his growing enterprise.

He loved her, but he had no illusions about his appearance. The scar faced him every time he shaved. It kept everyone at a distance, which wasn't so bad in his real business—protection. His real estate ventures were profitable, but he never forgot his vow to take care of his neighborhood, which to him meant protection—by whatever means necessary. His vast organization now thrived as residents, corporations, and even certain families paid for the kind of protection he could provide.

Maggie's job was to present the terms of residency to prospective clients and make them happy when they signed on the dotted line. He hoped she could train Claire to work with her. He had seen pictures of Claire and had periodic reports. But to keep her safe, he'd avoided meeting her directly. He made sure she was provided for, living with her grandmother. But her Nana was gone now, and he'd not heard much about Claire since she'd moved out on her own.

What would he do if Claire didn't work out? Casey would deal with that then. It might be a hard decision, but he had always made the difficult decisions. He truly hoped it wouldn't come to that. Well, that was for another day. Maggie would do what he asked. He could always count on her.

* * *

Maggie ushered Claire through the door of the little boutique. "Charmaine is a doll. Once she knows Casey foots the bill, nothing will be good enough for you," she said and gave a little laugh. "Let's have fun!"

Their day together progressed along the same lines: evening wear from the boutique, long gowns, and cocktail pantsuits for all the meet-and-greet occasions, another specialty store for the two custom-made suits for the day, made of the softest wool Claire had ever touched. The Jimmy Choo shoes were beyond thinking about.

"How are you enjoying your new apartment? Everything to your satisfaction?" Maggie's face was bright with anticipation.

Claire didn't answer at once. She put a hand on Maggie's arm and stopped, "Why is he doing all this? How do I repay all of it?" She had almost added, 'What does he want from me?'

Maggie looked at Claire quizzically. "Not to worry. He has plenty, and he likes sharing it."

"But it's so... so over the top!"

"Just be good at your job." She put her arm around Claire, and giving her a reassuring hug, she said, "My assignment is to make sure you are."

Why it all made Claire feel even more insecure, she wasn't sure. Certainly, it would be nice to have Maggie as a friend. She guessed she'd just go along and see how it all unfolded.

Claire became very good at her job. She loved meeting prospective clients, taking them to marvelous restaurants, watching as they signed on the dotted line! And the apartment, and the clothes! It was wonderful.

Once settled into her new job and vastly improved lifestyle, she finally was enjoying her new life. The only wrinkle was her feeling that a good-looking young man seemed to be stalking her.

One afternoon, he called out to Claire as she left her office. She turned to see who was calling her. "Yes?" she answered, recognizing this sharply dressed young man coming toward her. "How can I help you?" she asked somewhat nervously.

"I've been wanting to meet you," he said as he stopped in front of her. "I've been told that we are from the same neighborhood—Oh, sorry! I'm Bobby Roarke," he offered her his hand, which she did not take.

"I'm sorry, but—?"

"Maybe I've overstepped," Bobby hesitated. "But maybe we could have coffee sometime? Talk about who we know—or who we don't." He smiled at her, shrugging his shoulders in question.

Claire was a bit taken aback, but she also was somewhat charmed by his forward manner. "Maybe—" she started to say.

But he interrupted, "Great! I'll give you a call," and he took off, leaving her gawking after him.

That was how it began. Coffee, later a movie, then dinner followed by one night in her apartment that ended with breakfast the next morning. It was nice, but it wasn't going to go anywhere as far as she was concerned. Bobby felt too easy.

It was like the job. Some clients seemed—well— sort of dodgy. However, Maggie made it clear she didn't want to hear that. And Casey—he never talked to her at all!

She tried to put all her misgivings out of her mind. As the months went by, she told herself she would just have to learn to enjoy this incredible new life!

# CHAPTER 3

Working on the weekend when no one was around wasn't unusual for Claire. She leaned back in her ergonomic chair, stretching to get the kinks out of her shoulders. Goodness, it's already past four. She gazed out her office window and decided to enjoy the rest of the beautiful autumn day.

As she gathered the file she had been working on to put in her office safe, she smiled to herself, thinking, *Has it really been three years?* She shook her head as she gathered the rest of her things. Hard to believe, as she locked her door behind her.

Humming to herself, she left the elevator and moved toward the tall glass doors to exit the building. Suddenly she remembered her laptop. She needed it to finish up some loose ends on the report Maggie required by Monday.

Sighing, she turned around and took the elevator back up to her office. The building was always so quiet on the weekend.

As she searched for the key to her office, she heard what she thought were voices coming from Casey's corner office. The door was ajar, light spilling out. Curious, she quietly moved toward the sound of the strident voices.

Two men? She didn't recognize who was speaking—until another voice interrupted. Casey? The snatches of the argument she was catching were disturbing.

"HELL, NO! I won't just go along."

Mumbles came from the other man.

"I don't care who I have to hurt or walk over. I came for my cut, and that's what I intend to get."

She recognized his voice: Henry! The man yelling was Henry, her colleague—a real jerk, in her opinion. The unidentified man sharply cut him off. "Then, be aware, the only dead body will be yours!"

The light went out, and she heard movement. Casey was trying to urge the two adversaries out of his office. Claire quickly retreated back toward her own office. She simulated locking her already locked door.

"Claire! Why are you here?" exclaimed Casey as the three men came down the corridor toward her.

"Oh, Mr. Malone!" she sputtered. "I forgot something Maggie needs by Monday, so I came to pick it up." She smiled, probably too broadly to seem natural.

"Huh!" He paused and then said, "Well, don't work too hard." He ushered the two men past her and toward the elevator.

Her breathing finally slowed as she watched them leave. What was that all about? It shook her. Could Casey actually condone a killing? Maybe she had misunderstood. People do say things in anger that they don't really mean.

Still—the incident once again dredged up her apprehensions about some potential clients she met, especially at the meet-and-greet occasions. By the expensive clothes and the bejeweled women, it was evident that the common denominator was money. Everybody had lots of money. Maggie insisted she attend. It was part of her job, which was basically to be charming and beautiful. Sometimes it was fun. By now, it had become somewhat boring.

As she left the building, she realized she still didn't have her laptop. She hurried on. Monday would have to do.

* * *

After an uneasy weekend, Claire still got up Monday morning before her alarm. She had to finish that report, which meant getting to the office early. Dressing hurriedly, she turned on the TV to catch the local morning news. She was finishing her makeup when she heard a report of a man found dead in the Hudson River. She stopped. And turning, she focused on the image. "Oh, my god! It's him, Henry!" Her colleague.

She sat, stunned. Did Casey know that she had overheard their conversation? The threat?

Her fears escalated. No extravagant lifestyle was worth this fear. Casey had been so good, so generous with her. But she didn't really know him. Old fears she'd buried came roaring to the surface. Were the rumors about him true? Could he really be OK with murder? What if he realized she had heard them arguing? She gasped at what that might mean for her. She gulped. *I can't continue working there!*

She had to leave. But go where? Could she leave all this behind? She had to!

What if he ordered someone to make her disappear—if she didn't disappear on her own! But where could she go?

Suddenly, Claire thought of Lucky, and that lawyer she was dating. She knew what to do; she would see that attorney! But she had left his card on her office desk. She didn't want to risk running into Casey if she went back to the office.

*Chase! Was that his first name? Last name? I've got to talk to Lucky!* She grabbed her coat, purse, and keys. It would be a good idea to get more information about this attorney.

She hailed a cab and directed him to Lucky's place. Claire grabbed her cell phone. She fervently hoped Lucky was home.

Lucky was more than happy to have Claire stay for as long she wanted.

"I just wish we could hang out together," Lucky said. "But I have an audition for a touring company, and I will be gone for a few days."

Claire was hardly surprised at her friend's excitement. She'd been struggling with bit parts for a few years. This might be the breakthrough Lucky had longed for.

Actually, Claire was relieved that Lucky would be gone. She could handle the futon on the floor for a few days. It also gave Claire time to pack clothes and get other essentials from her apartment and decide what to do next.

Lucky gave her whatever information she knew about Dillon Chase as well as about his buddy, Max Morgan, a Private Detective. However, most of Lucky's information was about how cute Dillon was and how intimidating his partner, Max, seemed.

A few days after Lucky had left for her auditions, and Claire had settled into the tiny apartment, she was finally ready to meet Dillon Chase and his partner.

# CHAPTER 4

Dillon Chase, Esq. was apprehensive when he first got the call, requesting that he meet with Casey Malone. His first reaction was, *Why would he be calling me?* Followed by, *How did he get my number?*

It was later that he asked himself, *Why did I ever agree to work for Casey? Well, that's easy, the money!*

Dillon wasn't able to pay his past due bills, let alone the current ones. Still, according to rumors on the street, Casey was essentially a mob boss. Dillon's first glimpse of Malone's wealth was the high-rise glass building. He continued to be impressed as he approached a big guy, all in head-to-toe black, who beckoned him into his boss's office. *Was black garb required in mob-dom?*

With a deep breath to quiet his nerves, Dillon walked into the palatial room. A gigantic desk stood at the far end. *Was that some kind of dais that supported the high-backed chair?* In it, slouched Casey Malone.

Dillon stood before him. Casey looked up, waved at a chair, indicating that Dillon sit. He did.

Casey had been cagey. At first, he told Dillon just enough about his enterprises to whet his interest and then obtain a promise for his cooperation.

"Dillon! You don't mind if I call you Dillon?"

"Mr. Malone..."

"Casey will be fine. We're going to be friends. Right?"

"I don't think I understand—"

"Of course not. I haven't told you yet. I want you to find my... protege, Claire. She took off—took everything with her, and just scooted. We can't have that now, can we?"

"Mr. Malone, Casey, I'm an attorney. I don't have anything to do with missing persons."

"Not missing persons! A runaway!"

He gulped, but he had to ask, "And what exactly is her relationship to you?"

Malone cleared his throat before answering,

"She works for me. I told you. She's special; very special."

Dillon felt more and more uneasy, but asked anyway, "Uh, how old is she?"

"How old? I dunno—old enough to know too much—about my business!" He paused. "She's a looker. That's why I hired her."

"Mr. Mal—Casey, how did you get my name?"

"Your card. I saw it on her desk. Clever, huh? I figured she knew you, an attorney. And as her employer, I should know you too. See? So here you are—a nice looking chap—and now you can tell me where she is." He handed him a picture of Claire.

Later, when the actual 'job offer' became official, Dillon told Max, his almost-partner and best friend, about the deal. Max was skeptical about Casey's "projects," especially the part about finding Casey's 'protege,' especially when Dillon showed him the picture of Claire that Casey had given Dillon. Max only commented, "Pretty girl."

But Max understood. It was the money. Money enough for Dillon to open up a nicer office and create a legal business partnership with Max.

Blue-eyed, blond, tall Dillon, and lean, dark-complected, 6'3" Max met in Afghanistan. They were as unlikely a pair as one could imagine, and yet they had bonded almost immediately. After one tour together, they re-entered civilian life. Law school (thanks to his parents) for Dillon; a P.I. license for the less fortunate Max. Two years later, they formed an unofficial partnership—each complementing the other in their own fields.

However, things had become somewhat tense between them. It made it difficult for Dillon to ask Max for help. He hated to ask Max. But if anyone could find Claire for Casey, it would be Max.

But that was before they met Claire...

"Is this Dillon Chase's office?" asked Claire as she peaked around the partially open door.

"That's what the sign says, Miss.," Max said as he ushered her into the office. "This is Mr. Chase behind the desk. And I am Max," he said as he indicated she could sit in the chair beside his.

As she tentatively entered and then sat, Max raised a quizzical eyebrow. Did Dillon recognize her? Max couldn't help but wonder why this beautiful and expensively dressed woman was coming to this office.

Dillon gave a start as he realized that this was Claire from the picture Casey had given him. He gave Max a look of *don't blow it* as he rose and extended his hand to Claire. "And you are?" he asked.

Claire rose again to take his hand as she answered, "Claire Cousins. A friend suggested I call you—uh—which I know I didn't do, call you, I mean." She stopped abruptly, sat once again, cleared her throat. "I'm hoping you can help me."

"And what is it exactly that you need, Miss. Cousins?"

"Oh, please, call me Claire." Then, a little embarrassed, added, "This Miss. and Mr. business makes me a little nervous."

"All right, Claire, tell me—us," indicating Max, "what is on your mind?"

Claire paused as she took a longer look at the dark, handsome man who remained standing, arms folded and staring at her. "It's sort of an unusual situation—and—all this is confidential, right?"

Max spoke up, "You have a dollar bill, Claire?"

"Yes, sure. I think so." She pulled out a wallet and fished out a one-dollar bill.

"Now just give that to Dillon, you become his client, and all conversations, transactions are totally confidential. OK?" He had a trace of a smile on his face.

Claire reached across the desk with the dollar bill and handed it to Dillon with a glance at Max, who she found very attractive. She admonished herself to stick to business.

Dillon found himself quite drawn to this well-put-together young woman, but he, too, was wondering what she was doing in his tiny office. Her dress, hair, careful makeup said money. *So, why has she chosen to come here?*

"Why don't you just start from the beginning, and we'll determine how we can help you." He was very curious to hear her story.

"I think he is—do you know the name, Casey Malone?" Dillon and Max exchanged glances as they nodded in reply to her question. "Well, I work for him—or I did—and if he knew that I disclosed anything about his business," she hesitated, "I don't kn... that is, I'm afraid... He did warn me when I first met him..." She stopped, anxiously wringing her hands, not sure what she wanted to say to these two men who kept staring at her.

Max asked, "Why don't you go to the police or even the FBI?"

"No! No. I couldn't! Oh, dear. I shouldn't have come," she said as she rose to leave. "Thank you. I am so sorry to have bothered you."

Max reached his hand out to her. "Please wait. Anything you tell us will be confidential, remember?"

She slowly sat back down. "It's just that I am unsure..."

Dillon spoke, "Just tell us what disturbs you."

Claire explained her growing misgivings about the people she met and the argument she had overheard. Finally, she told them about her colleague, who was found in the Hudson River. Her fear was palpable. She was afraid of what might happen to her if Casey knew she had been listening.

"I know this will sound strange. But I just want to disappear, to get away where he can't find me." She paused, looking down at her hands tightly clasped. "He's been good to me," she emphasized. "Very generous. But I don't think anything would stop him if he thought I betrayed his trust. I don't want to hurt him; I just want to get myself free...

from any obligations. What if he comes after me?"

They could see that her fear was real.

"I have money to pay you—thanks to him, really. So?"

"Complicated," said Dillon as he exchanged a look with Max.

"Where are you staying now?" Max asked. "How do we reach you?"

Claire wrote down a phone number. She had bought a burner phone for this purpose. "I'm with a friend for a couple of days, but I have to be gone as soon as possible. So, can you help me?"

"We'll get back to you by tonight," Dillon assured her. He caught Max's lifted eyebrow. "We'll see what we can do."

She rose, straightening her skirt. "Thank you. And be sure to tell me what this will cost," she said anxiously.

"Of course, until this evening."

As the door closed, Max looked at Dillon, "A plan?"

"We can do *something*, Max. She said she can pay us."

"Do you not realize that we have a conflict of interest here?"

"Max! She's in danger. Doesn't that override Casey's wanting to find her?"

Max stood, looking at Dillon. He shrugged his shoulders as a 'yes.'

"And she asked *how much*," smiled Dillon.

"I know, I know." Max paused, thinking. "OK. Let's start with getting Frank as her bodyguard. He's reliable. What if..." He took another moment. "Her only leverage is what she knows about Malone's dealings. And she doesn't want to use it."

"Yeah, but Casey doesn't know that." Dillon continued, "Look! What if we convince her to give a deposition on tape, that we hold as insurance; a threat; no, a deterrent!"

"That might actually buy her the time she needs to get away. Where do we come in?" asked Max.

"We set up the deposition, and *maybe*... let Casey know we've heard rumors about *someone* going to the FBI. He'd buy that. I'll bet that's what he's afraid of."

"Could be dangerous." Max paced. "We can get her a new identity, then she buys a ticket to wherever—only she knows where—and we're done."

"OK, Max, let's get going. I'll set up the

deposition in that new high-rise downtown. You get the papers for identity change; we already have her picture. Can you get a hold of Frank? And check out the cost to rent a Lincoln. That gets us started. I'll talk to her this evening." Dillon picked up the phone, ready to put the plan into action.

Max stopped him, "What do we tell Casey?"

"Nothing! Not now. Not yet."

"OK, Dillon. We'll do it your way—for now." He took a breath, shrugged his shoulders. "Do let her know what this will cost her—a high figure to give us a profit for a change. We can always negotiate."

"OK, OK. Let's get going," Dillon said, starting to dial.

Max didn't feel easy with working for Casey. And considering the money involved, Dillon had agreed he should have asked, or at least researched more. But the advance from Casey had kept Dillon's office functioning. There even was enough money for them to consider that real partnership with Max that Dillon kept talking about.

And what about this Claire? Casey's 'protege'? Even Dillon had questions. What if she didn't want to be 'found'? Were they obligated to reveal her whereabouts to Casey, or were they primarily obligated to Claire?

"What do you think about Claire? I mean—is she for real?" Dillon asked.

"As much as you or me, I suppose." Max shrugged.

"Meaning?"

"Come on," Max said. "Were we upfront with her? Obviously, she doesn't know Malone hired us."

"That's different. Need-to-know and all that."

"Sure, Dillon."

"I think Casey cares about her, don't you? But you have to wonder. If it's platonic, I mean." Dillon looked at Max's skeptical expression. "She's gorgeous!"

"So what if it isn't? Or is, for that matter? How does that matter to us—or to you?"

"OK," Dillon said.

"OK? Look, you're attracted to her. I get that. But isn't it better to hold off until we know exactly which side we're on?" Max asked.

"Yeah—sure. I know you're right." Dillon nodded. "Casey was so vague about their relationship. It's just hard to put this all together.

Is she in trouble? Or is she over-reacting?

"Not enough pieces to put anything together yet. Let it lie."

Max's common sense told him that anyone connected to Casey Malone had danger all over them. But Dillon was like that—impulsive, ready for any new challenge. Same in Afghanistan— almost got both of them killed.

# CHAPTER 5

Dillon got back to her, as promised. When he explained that she had to give a deposition, her anxiety escalated. It took a while to convince her it was the only way. It was set for tomorrow morning. He arranged to have her picked up. Frank, the bodyguard, would be beside her all the way.

If only she wasn't so scared.

Claire awoke that morning, nervous, but full of hope. Even the thought of having a bodyguard hovering was just a minor irritant. She would get this deposition done, and then she would be free! She would hop a plane to—*Aruba!* Those trailers on TV made it seem so heavenly. She sighed. Actually, any place was better than here right now.

She showered quickly and dressed as planned: navy blue linen suit, light blue silk blouse—the dreaded high heels. Not exactly the casual but elegant pants suits she preferred for work. But she had to dress the part, after all.

She smiled as she considered her makeup. A light touch today, she thought. Her light brown hair with the gold highlights pulled back into a chignon would complete the image she was after. *Small pearl earrings—hm—too obvious, maybe?* Better the silver loops. A strong cup of coffee and she was ready for whatever the day would bring.

Frank, her assigned bodyguard, met her at the door, exactly on time, as Dillon had promised. When she asked about Dillon, he told her that Dillon would meet them at the top of the plaza stairs. The black Lincoln town car was idling in front of her building.

Unused to the tight skirt and heels, she carefully got into the car, settled back as Frank took the driver's seat. "Feels like a Mafia car," she muttered to herself, as Frank pulled away.

Frank hurried her out of the car.

When she didn't see Dillon, she asked,

"Shouldn't we wait for Dillon to arrive?"

Shaking his head, he urged her to walk faster toward the stairs.

Frank was close now, right behind her. She quickened her steps, anxious to get this whole experience behind her. She hadn't anticipated needing a bodyguard; it seemed excessive. As they crossed the plaza, she noted that Frank had moved up beside her, shielding her from the street, she guessed.

*Why must I do this; how did they talk me into this—a deposition?* she thought. Breath coming more quickly now. Her heels were higher than she usually tolerated. The stockings were so annoying on such a hot day.

Shots rang out—*pop, pop.*

Frank grabbed her arm, pulling her to him, forcing her to run. The plaza stretched out ahead of them—so far to the tall glass doors. Where did the shots come from? Who were they shooting at?

More shots.

Suddenly Frank's grip was gone; he fell to the pavement, causing her to stumble.

He yelled at her, "*RUN!*"

Another shot!

She couldn't stop! She was back on her feet. She ran as best she could in the tight skirt and high heels. She staggered at last into the heavy glass door, pushing it away from her, hoping it was bulletproof. Where could she hide?

Another *pop, pop.* This time hitting the glass doors. They held!

*They're after me!* her mind screamed. *Got to find a way out.*

Crowds of workers and visitors poured into the lobby of the building. She removed her navy blue jacket as she moved toward them, hoping her pale blue silk blouse would make her less recognizable in the crowd.

She edged her way around people, toward the elevator.

A man stood still in front of her escape route—looking for her? *Can't take a chance,* she whispered to herself. *Where? A sign to the cafeteria!* Maybe a back door to a loading dock.

She walked quickly, unnoticed in the milling crowd, moving—and there was the door! She eased through, running through the kitchen, then out the door that led to an alley.

*Which way to turn? The park!* The long

driveway leading away from the building led her into the park. Claire's breathing grew ragged.

*There!* A bench was almost hidden behind foliage. She needed to stop, catch her breath.

Claire collapsed onto the bench, bent over, her hands on her knees as she slowed her breathing. Her thoughts were going in all directions. *Were they really after me?*

Without thinking, she pulled off her shoes, then leaned back, trying to recover. Shaking, as the adrenaline started oozing away, she fussed. *This must be shock.* The idea that someone could have been shooting at her began to feel ridiculous. *Did I overreact? Why am I always running? No one was actually chasing me and out to get me. How would Casey even know?*

Her breath was finally slowing down. Her recurring memory of long ago fading; *the gang after her... almost caught her...*

Abruptly, she straightened up. Adrenaline shot through her again. She had been so scared she forgot about Frank! She relived that moment he was no longer by her side.

*What happened to Frank? He got shot! He fell. And I just kept running! Should I go back? The shooting... he must have been shot. Protecting me! From what? From whom?*

The more she thought, the more her anxiety turned to anger. *Where in the hell was Dillon? Some attorney he turned out to be. Didn't even show up! Why had he insisted on a bodyguard?*

Claire couldn't sit any longer. As she bent to pull on her shoes, she noticed someone staring at her. Her shoes back on, and as casually as she could, she rose.

Should she go back to the office building? The police would want to talk to her. *Not the police!* She began walking along the path which meandered through overgrown shrubs and trees. *Where was the way out?*

*There!* An exit onto a busy pedestrian way, and a small coffee house just beyond. She practically sprinted toward it. Once inside, she took a corner table from where she could see anyone enter. The kitchen door was right next to it.

She felt frozen, unable to think, let alone act. When the waiter approached, she mumbled out, "A latte, please."

\* \* \*

Dillon Chase, Esq. stood beside his car, stunned at the chaos he saw throughout the plaza. What had happened to Claire? And what had happened to Frank, her bodyguard?

Traffic had blocked his access to the office building, so he had arrived a lot later than he had promised Claire.

Police were surrounding the building and plaza with crime tape. His eyes were drawn to the body in the center of the plaza. He took a sharp breath as he watched the paramedics, lifting it onto a stretcher—not a body bag. He hoped that was good.

He pushed his way through the crowd to a policeman guarding the perimeter. He extended his ID toward him as he asked, "What happened here?"

Dillon drove away from the plaza, heading back to his office, regretting his promise to Claire that she would be protected; she wouldn't be in danger. She just had to show up at the rented office, give her deposition, and split—if that is what she wanted to do. He had thought a deposition, telling all she knew about her boss, Casey Malone, would protect all of them. He certainly didn't plan to give it to anyone, unless, of course, they were threatened.

He couldn't help thinking that all this had begun in the first place with agreeing to work for Casey Malone. Why had he ever agreed to work for Casey? The money sure wasn't enough to get shot at.

His concern wasn't just for Claire or Frank. What was he going to tell Casey? How did he get himself into this mess? The strangest part was the request, order really, to find his 'protege.' Had Casey somehow found out about Claire's deposition? That possibility put a knot in his gut.

He hadn't even got started with Claire. A charm offensive was in his repertoire, but so far, nothing had worked.

At least, he convinced her to do a deposition, which he would keep safely hidden.

But an assassination attempt? Was the gunman after Claire, or maybe it had been random?

\* \* \*

Claire called Dillon's cell phone number. It rang only once before he picked up, his relief palpable, "Claire, where in the hell are you?"

"Frank was shot!" Her voice choked up with sudden unshed tears. *Did he have any idea what she had just been through?*

"Are you OK?"

Aware of the waiter listening, she whispered into her phone, "Didn't you hear what I said? Frank may be dead!"

"I don't think so. I think I saw the paramedics put him on a gurney."

"Where *were* you?! You promised to meet us on the stairs!"

Dillon tried to calm her, "I'll explain everything, but right now—"

She broke in, "I don't dare use my plane reservation." By now, her tears were flowing.

"So, you were going to split."

"Of course, I am going to split! You were supposed to help me get away! I'm certainly not going to hang around waiting for Casey Malone or anyone else to find me—"

He cut her off, "We don't know that this was Casey—"

"Those bullets sure seemed close to me, or was someone after your guy, Frank?" She stuffed her tears. "You said I wouldn't be in danger, but you still had to make sure I had a bodyguard who is shot, dying because of me!"

"We don't know that for sure. Please, just calm down. Maybe after you make the deposition—"

"I'm out of here, Dillon, with or without the stupid deposition *or* your help." Claire hung up and quickly exited through the cafe's kitchen door. People stared, but no one yelled at her as she hurried into the alley.

She'd grab a cab, pick up her bags at Lucky's...

She stopped, realizing that Casey might know about Lucky's. If it was him...

Claire didn't know for sure that someone was shooting at *her—specifically*. She felt terrible about Frank. He was just trying to protect her.

She started walking again; no destination in mind.

Maybe she *could* get that plane ticket. Aruba sure sounded glorious right now.

*What was Dillon really about? He kept pushing for her to make a deposition about Casey Malone, her boss. He said it was for protection. For*

*Herself? Dillon? Max?*

*All she wanted was a safe haven. At least until she figured out the rest of her life!*

\* \* \*

Once back in his office, Dillon picked up the desk phone, started to tap 911, then slammed it down. *Where was she?* He paced, glancing from time to time at the muted TV, watching for any news. Again, he grabbed the phone, but this time quick-dialed Max.

Max hung up his phone, grabbed his wallet, and took off—once again, to take care of Dillon's mess. He had a pretty good idea about where to look for Claire. The streets leading away from the plaza were a good place to start.

Max slowed down his car as he neared the plaza, his eyes alert as he searched the streets for Claire. A few seconds later, he spotted her as she rounded the corner from an alley. He pulled up in front of her, got out, threw open the passenger door, and told her to get in fast.

Overcoming her initial panic, Claire got in as

soon as she realized it was Max. He wasted no time in pulling away. Both were quiet, and Claire's heavy breathing finally calmed down. Max focused on getting them both to safety.

Once underway, he grabbed his cell phone and quick-dialed Dillon: "I have Claire; we're on our way," said Max and disconnected.

The town car moved smoothly through the side streets, avoiding the usually clogged highways. At last, Claire began to feel safe, nestled in the deep cushions. No bar in this fancy car, though. And she could really use a drink!

As she settled down her thoughts turned to Dillon. *Why did he take me on? He hasn't made a dime in that so-called law office, not that I can see, anyway. Hm. The bodyguard, the car?* She cringed as she thought about Frank; it could have been her if he hadn't moved up beside her.

Her nerves, still unraveling, she asked, "Max, why isn't there a portable bar in here?"

"Because Dillon doesn't drink, and he doesn't like sloppy clients."

*Oh, brother*, she thought to herself. *How am I going to get through this?*

After a bit, she sweetly as possible asked, "Max,

would you just tell me where we are going?"

"We're meeting up at the office. He wants to regroup. You scared him."

*Was that good or not?* she thought. At least she was safe—for the moment. She figured that was all she was going to hear from Max.

*Why was he so stoic? When he smiled, he seemed so charming.* She took a deep breath, trying to relax. Still, she couldn't stop fretting about her situation. Was she the target? And if so, were they still after her?

# CHAPTER 6

*Where the hell was Max?* Dillon resumed his nervous pacing. *He should be here by now.* About to pick up his phone once again, he heard loud footsteps.

Dillon stood as Claire came storming into the office, frantic, "Why am I here, Dillon? You are supposed to get me to a safe place. Do you think nobody knows about this rinky-dink operation? Come on, you have to do better than this!"

"Just take it easy, Claire. Here, sit down. There is no reason anyone would look for you here. He has no idea we've ever met."

"*He?* You are talking about Casey, aren't you? You think he—Oh my god!" She collapsed into a chair by the desk. "Of course! He must know about the deposition... That's why he was able to find me this morning."

Her face had lost all color as the realization swept over her. "Did *you* set me up? He shot at me, Dillon!"

"I don't think *he* was the one shooting," Max quipped as he came through the door.

Through angry tears, she snorted, "Oh, that is very funny!" Sarcastically, she added, "Of course, he would hire a gun to do the *dirty* work." She paused, grabbing a tissue from her bag. "The point is he knew I would be there and when. How did he know that? Huh—How?"

"Claire, we would never—"

"Oh, don't try to sweet-talk me!" She attempted to lower her voice, "Fine, it wasn't you." Then, after taking an exacerbated breath, she said, "Just give me the plan—you have a plan, right?"

"Well, things have changed a bit since this morning. No, don't say anything for just a minute," Dillon tried to placate her, "The important thing is that you got away. Now, we can take the next step."

"And what step would that be?"

Standing behind her as he followed this interchange, Max just shook his head, turned away, and crossed to the window. Looking down through the office window, he noticed a crowd gathering across the street. What was going on? People were pushing their way into the coffee shop, actually running... from what? "Dillon, come here! Look! Down at the street!"

"Oh shit!"

"Yeah, right! That *could be* Casey's entourage."

Panicking, Claire rushed to the window. "His what? Who? How do you know that? Is that why Max brought me here? Oh, man! You double-crossing heels! You betrayed me; you have been lying to me ever since I met you!"

She started to move toward the door, but Dillon grabbed her arm.

"No, Claire. I swear. We truly want to help you, but right now, we have to get out of here."

She was too scared to resist.

Shouting at Max to get the closed sign on the door, he grabbed his briefcase and marched her to the connecting door leading downstairs that was hidden behind a false bookcase.

Max had already headed out the office door and down the back stairs.

As they hurried, Dillon grabbed the cell phone from his pocket and fast dialed Max: "Get the car.

Meet us at the back—"

"Already on it," Max replied. "I'm there. Hurry!"

As he waited for Dillon and Claire, Max got the car running. He couldn't stop his anxious tapping on the steering wheel. He wished he could shout at Dillon. *What happened to a small but lucrative case that would at most take a couple of days? This reminds me far too much of our adventures in Afghanistan!*

Max was not looking for more adventure; he was working on an exit plan for himself, away from Casey and most likely from Dillon. Apparently, that was on hold for the time being.

# CHAPTER 7

Once they were in the car, Max careened through the alley and headed for the nearby expressway. He was fast but careful.

Claire and Dillon sat, not moving, not talking. Stunned.

Once out of the City, Max slowed down and glanced at them through the rearview mirror. He broke the ice, "We're heading to a place I know— no, Dillon, you don't know about this place."

Abruptly, Max pulled into a rest stop. "Wait here," he instructed as he quickly got out.

"Where are we?" Claire asked. "What's he doing out there?"

Dillon kept his eyes on Max, who seemed to be searching for something on the car or under the car. "Damn, he thinks we may have a tracker!

Claire, check your cushions and all around you."

"For what? What am I looking for?"

"A button or anything that looks different or out of place."

"I don't see anything. Dillon." Claire grabbed his arm. "Dillon! Look at me. Be honest. Does Casey know something about you and me? Why would he track *your* car?" Her voice was becoming shrill with her fear as well as her anger.

Max opened the car door, got in, and stopped her growing tirade with a look. Very calmly, he accelerated and regained the expressway. "No tracker I could find. How about you, Dillon? Any funny hardware that shouldn't be there?"

"Nothing. I think we're clean."

"Claire," Max grabbed her attention with his voice. "Please keep quiet. I need to focus and make sure we aren't being tailed. I know you are scared, but I am getting all of us to a safer place. I'll explain everything then."

Dillon leaned toward Max and said, "I don't know where—"

"I do, Dillon. Just let it rest."

# CHAPTER 8

After driving highways, twisty back roads, and a couple of dirt ones, Max pulled up next to a small cabin. He paused, checked the surroundings, and then circled around to the back where he parked amid tall brush and overhanging trees.

"Everyone out," Max barked as he headed for the cellar door of the cabin. As he investigated the lock, he ascertained that it hadn't been tampered with.

He unlocked the cellar door: "OK, folks, inside."

Dillon and Claire paused before entering into a large room.

"Not exactly a cellar," Dillon muttered.

They went down the few stairs into what appeared to be a fully furnished studio apartment. There was a bed in one corner and a sofa against the opposing wall. Two recliners were set in front of a small fireplace. Bookshelves filled with paperbacks flanked the fireplace, and what appeared to be an entertainment center took up another wall. There was also a small dining table with chairs around it. Truly a "safe" house for someone who expected to stay awhile.

Claire had no sense of where they were. The back roads had totally skewed her sense of direction.

Dillon had already plopped himself into one of the recliners.

She looked with concern around the room, and then she fixed her stare at Max, puzzlement on her face. He stood, watching *her* as well.

Max responded to her look. "As you can see, we are in a pretty secluded place. You can feel safe here, Claire, at least for the time being." He was doing his best to be reassuring.

"Safe? From whom? Casey? Dillon? You?"

"I'll explain what we know, Claire. But let's get settled first." He indicated a door in the back of the room, "That door leads to a kitchen and a small bathroom. Make yourself as comfortable as you can. I'll make us some coffee," he said as he headed toward the kitchen.

"I think I'd rather have a whiskey!" she fumed.

"Coffee is better—for now," Max smiled as he started toward the door. He paused, then turned toward her: "Oh, cream? Sugar?"

Claire choked out her answer: "Black!" which certainly matched her mood.

Max returned with a tray holding three mugs and spoons and set out a pitcher of cream and a bowl of sugar on the table. Claire huddled on the couch with a blanket wrapped around her shoulders. Dillon snored lightly in his recliner.

Max apologized: "Sorry for the cold. But smoke from a fire in the fireplace might alert unwelcome visitors." He handed the mug of black coffee to Claire. He looked at the two exhausted travelers. Where to begin, he thought. Maybe the so-called revelations could wait until tomorrow when everyone had some rest. That is if Claire was tired enough to agree. She was an enigma to him. Angry, but also very vulnerable beneath her bravado. Maybe it was that vulnerability that attracted him... In spite of himself.

"Why don't you take the bed," he suggested. "I'll sleep on the couch. Dillon seems comfortable enough in his recliner. We can talk in the morning."

Claire slowly sipped the hot coffee, tired beyond her imagining. She just nodded, pulled the blanket close around her, put the mug on the table, and headed for the bed.

Max quietly stood and made the rounds to all the alert monitors hidden in the room. Once assured they were activated, he found a blanket for himself and lay on the couch, finally falling into a light doze.

* * *

"RUN! RUN!" Frank, her bodyguard, was screaming at her. "RUN!"

She choked out, "I AM RUNNING!"

The huge glass doors beckoned. Why must I do this? How did they talk me into this? Her chest was heaving, trying to get enough breath to keep running.

More Shots—pop, pop—rang out.

Suddenly Frank's grip was gone. Where was Frank? Where were the shots coming from? WHY ARE THEY SHOOTING AT ME!

*FRANK SCREAMED AT HER: "RUN!"* Her voice filled the room, her body twitching as she sat straight up.

Max jolted awake, concerned. He approached her bed, "Shh, shh..." He wrapped his arms around her, pulling her close, shushing her, reassuring her that she was safe. Eventually, she quieted, and he gently lay her back down on the bed, where she seemed to fall into a deeper, more peaceful sleep.

Max found sleep impossible. He was affected by her vulnerability, which surprised him. He wanted to dismiss his feelings, but he couldn't quite shake them off.

In the morning, Claire opened her eyes, trying to figure out where she was. Slowly, she sat up and straightened her clothes. Gratefully, she smelled the brewing coffee, *and was that bacon?*

Max was pouring fresh orange juice as Claire walked over to the table set for breakfast: scrambled eggs, toast, and a server with bacon.

He wondered if she remembered her nightmare. It was obvious she had been traumatized by the shooting. Max had seen similar reactions on the battlefield.

Hoping for a mellower mood, he smiled, "I thought a late breakfast might be in order this morning."

"I'll have more appetite when I know what in the hell is going on," was her curt response.

Hiding his disappointment, he calmly replied, "All in good time."

Claire gritted her teeth.

"Dillon, get your lazy body over here," Max said. "Breakfast is ready, but it isn't served."

"You're certainly jovial this morning," Dillon grumbled as he left the recliner and sat down at the table. He poured himself a cup of coffee. "Claire? Coffee?"

"I'll pour my own, thank you," she said tersely.

"Oh, boy—" Dillon began.

"Leave her be," interrupted Max. "She had a rough night."

Claire looked at him. "What exactly are you talking about?"

"It's not uncommon to have nightmares when you have been traumatized."

Claire ignited and hurled at him: "What do you

know about being traumatized!"

Quietly, Max said, "Dillon and I were in Afghanistan. We both know more about being attacked than we would like. And yes, even soldiers have nightmares."

Without asking her, he poured her a cup of coffee and moved the cream in her direction. He then sat close to her. "You don't remember anything about your dream?"

Claire shook her head, sitting very still.

"I've found that talking about it helps," Max said, "I don't know how I would have gotten through that time without Dillon."

"Were you wounded?" Claire asked sheepishly.

"No. Came close a few times, but we were luckier than many."

Claire looked up at him quizzically.

Max got up and cleared his plate. "We all need to eat and then get down to brass tacks," he said.

"What does that even mean?" queried Claire.

"Sooner we finish, the sooner the revelations can begin." He smiled at her.

Claire was uneasy as she sat and sipped the strong coffee, ignoring the food on the table. She pondered, *Who were these men?* She felt stupid or at least very naïve to have put herself in their hands with little or no knowledge of who they really were. *That was her pattern, wasn't it?* she thought to herself. Trust but forget to verify.

It was becoming clear that it wasn't Dillon who was in charge; it was Max. *How did I miss that,* she wondered. *And what did he mean, she had a rough night?*

She vaguely remembered she had awakened with a feeling of panic, but then being able to go back to sleep.

*Her friend, Lucky, had vouched for them, but what did Lucky really know about either man? Dillon was the talker, not surprising for an attorney. Max? Very stoic; he gave no clues to what he was really thinking. He certainly didn't seem very friendly. Then out of the blue, Max seemed concerned. He even smiled at her.*

She took another sip of her coffee and then snagged a piece of bacon.

Her feelings about Max were mixed: *He was the one who got them away.* She actually felt safe with him. She shook her head slightly and continued sipping the welcome coffee.

Why hadn't she paid attention to her misgivings about Casey right at the beginning? Before just jumping at the goodies offered? She *knew* it was all too good to be true! But what she could never figure out was what he wanted from her? Could Casey really be the one who wanted *to kill* her?

Uncomfortably, she remembered Casey's warning when she first met him in the limo: anything about his business was never to be revealed to anyone. And she had already revealed to these two men that terrible conversation she overheard.

She couldn't get out of her mind the image of Henry being pulled from the Hudson River. She had planned to be very careful about what she would say on the deposition.

Why had she listened to Dillon? *A deposition, for goodness' sake!* Well, the one good thing was her instinct to leave the company. A huge sigh escaped her lips unconsciously.

The men noticed.

"Just a headache coming on," she lied.

What had she been thinking? Well, that was the problem: she wasn't thinking; she was running for her life.

There was something suspicious about them. She had to get away from these two—even if that meant just going for a walk. Maybe she could figure out where in the heck she was. She pulled her chair away from the table, grabbed the blanket from the bed, wrapped it around her, and started for the door.

Max interrupted her exit, calling, "There's a jacket in the closet that should fit. A lot more comfortable." He watched her as she stopped, turned, and headed in the direction Max had indicated. She retrieved one of the down jackets hanging there and noticed a pair of gloves on the upper shelf.

"OK if I use these, too?" she asked with raised eyebrows.

"Sure, just be sure you return them," he pointedly told her as he watched her leave.

*What was with this lady?* Max asked himself. *First, she wants our help and then acts as if we are against her. And why should I care so much?* He shook his head and then turned to Dillon. "Are you finished yet?"

Dillon pushed back his chair from the table.

Looking at Max, and in a somewhat belligerent tone, he asked, "You seem to have taken over. What do you have in mind?"

Max just shrugged, "I guess someone had to take charge."

There was a long pause. Dillon rose and walked around the room, smoldering. Finally, he stopped in front of Max. "I don't get you, man. You bring us out here—wherever—'here' is; no discussion, no—"

Max stayed seated as he cut him off, "Your downfall has always been beautiful women. Gotta rescue the damsel in distress, and off you go on your charger—and then yell for Max to come get your ass out of whatever mess you've landed in."

"That's not fair, Max!" His voice getting louder.

"As I remember, there was an incident with Suzanna in Paris, and then—what was her name—Gretchen, was it, in Germany," Max's voice matched Dillon's.

"True. But we were on our way home and—"

"But we BOTH might not ever have got home without a little interference from good ol' Max."

"Come on!" Dillon threw his hands in the air. "That's old stuff!"

"Oh? And exactly what is your plan for the three

of us *now*, Dillon? When were you going to tell Claire that we have been working for Casey before we even met her! And who in the hell is Claire Cousins, anyway? Just how deep is she in Casey's so-called business? And—"

The door banged open.

Claire entered, furious at what she just had overheard. "No problem, gentlemen! I've got a ride out of here! Bobby said he could get here by afternoon." She added, "He checked the GPS on my phone."

Her smug smile disappeared at their reaction.

Both Max and Dillon shouted, "PHONE!" They looked at each other with agitation and began stammering at each other that the other idiot should have retrieved Claire's phone.

Claire tried to interrupt, "What's wrong with you two? Bobby is a good guy. He'd do anything for me. Which is certainly more than I can say for either of you!"

The shouting stopped. No one looked at anyone.

Dillon let out a huge breath, "Claire, who is Bobby?"

"He's a friend, and he's working out a way to get

me on a plane." Trying to stay upbeat, "See, that leaves the two of you out of it!" Her chirpy tone wasn't very convincing.

Max held up his hand: "Claire, again, who is Bobby?"

"I told you, he's a friend... sort of a boyfriend." She averted her eyes.

Max coughed to stop Dillon from saying anything. But Dillon said it anyway, "How come you haven't said anything about him before?"

She felt caught by her own story. "I, uh, I just didn't want to involve him or encourage him to think—" She stopped mid-sentence, unsure... She looked at the two intense men staring at her. "I didn't think you would understand."

Dillon asked, "Understand what?"

"Why I didn't ask him to help me in the beginning."

Max asked this time, "And why was that, Claire?"

She squirmed as she got out of the jacket and walked to the closet, "He works for Casey." She turned abruptly, and in their faces said, "Just like the two of you!"

"And now? Why did you call him *now*?" Max

insisted.

"Because... Look, I really appreciate your getting me away. But I don't know either of you or if I can trust you! Good grief, I'm just finding out you work for Casey. And not because you told me yourselves!"

Max tried to interrupt her, "Claire—"

"Anyway," she cut him off sharply, then modulated her tone, "I'm sure you want to be free of me as soon as possible. So, I called Bobby." She paused as she looked at their expressions. "I'll be happy to write you a check. So, no problem."

Max held out his hand to her. "Give me the phone, Claire."

Frustrated, she clung to the phone, before she sheepishly handed it to him.

"OK, group," Max directed. "Pack up the food. Gather up your stuff. We are out of here. Now!" He started closing down the monitors, setting the alarm, and transporting some of the food as well as blankets to the car.

Claire just stood watching him, her mouth open with unasked questions.

"Come on, Claire, let's move!" Dillon had already started loading up the car with provisions, getting the urgency.

As Claire was being urged into the car, she yelped, "But what about Bobby?" Angrily, she allowed herself to be buckled in and wondered, *what was the matter with these guys? Maybe they were the ones to be afraid of. Where was Max taking them?*

As Dillon started getting into the front seat next to Max, he could see how agitated she was becoming: "Listen, Claire, if Bobby works for Casey, then you can be sure Casey knows where you are." He caught the skeptical look on her face. "I know, we also work for Casey—but we also had misgivings, especially after hearing your story."

Max accelerated onto the road. At Dillon's quick glance, he acknowledged him with a nod to tell her everything.

"We absolutely did not tell him where you are, even though he wanted us to find you," Dillon explained.

Claire didn't know how to take in that last bit of information. She pleaded, "At least, let me call Bobby and tell him not to come." She got no response. She protested loudly, "I want my phone back!"

Max unsuccessfully tried to appease her, "Please, Claire! Try to understand—"

"I want out, right now! Stop the car! Let me out!"

Firmly, holding back his growing anger, Max said, "Can't do that, Claire." He kept on driving. As they approached a narrow bridge that spanned a deep ravine, he slowed the car, opened his window, and tossed the phone over the barrier into the deep crevasse.

Watching the phone sail over the bridge railing into the deep space below, Claire was shocked into silence. Tears were running down her face, but she made no noise.

Glancing back at her, Dillon said, "It's going to be fine. It will all work out."

Max focused on navigating the twisting dirt roads. It would be awhile before the car would be humming along a paved highway. No conversation. No one except Max knew where they were headed.

Eventually, wiping away her tears, Claire said quietly, "I have no cash. Just credit cards, which I suppose you won't let me use." No one responded. "I can write you a check! So, you should just let me out in the next town." No response. In as enthusiastic a voice she could muster, "You'll be rid of me; no one will be after you!"

Max smiled as he drove. "Nice try, Claire, but no can do."

"Why not?" was her anguished reply.

"We are all in this together, whether we want to be or not."

# CHAPTER 9

Bobby got off the call from Claire. He had assured her he could find her by tracking her phone. He grabbed his keys and left for the cabin she described. While running for his truck, he tried to figure out how he was going to square this with Sam. *And Casey! He must not get wind of this!* He had to make sure Casey had no inkling that there was a mole (named Bobby!) in his organization.

For the first time that he could recall, a woman had made him want to be someone else, someone Claire could love. *Why did this have to happen to me now?*

What if the bodyguard hadn't moved beside her just as he took the shot? She would be dead. But instead, she had *reached out to him*. She was in trouble. He had to protect her—ironically, from himself. How was he going to do that?

When he first met Claire, Bobby figured he'd hit the jackpot. The unexpected prize was when he overheard Maggie referring to Claire as Casey's protege. Sam was delighted when Bobby told him that. Finally, Sam had the means to hurt Casey, where he was emotionally vulnerable.

Sam ordered him to get close to her, find out what she knew, then get rid of her. "It will stab Casey in the heart!" Sam had chortled.

Bobby had been ecstatic: To be trusted as Sam's Hit Man! His reputation would hit the ceiling, and the bonus promised? Oh, yeah. That would put him on easy street for sure.

Getting close to a beautiful woman was the easy part. Bobby had no difficulty in the Ladies' Department. Not with his Black Irish looks: the piercing blue eyes and wavy black hair. He knew he was brash, but women seemed to like it. Throw them a line and reel them in.

That is—before he saw Claire.

It was all Sam's fault! It got all screwed up because Sam was hell-bent on hurting Casey. What a mess.

What was all that about, anyway? He'd never

asked that before—about any job for which he had been hired. Bobby was not used to complicated relationships. His way was simple: find the target, shoot—never miss—and get out pronto.

# CHAPTER 10

It was late afternoon by the time they left the dirt roads behind them and got onto an expressway. Max drove into the first rest area they came to and stopped at the gas pumps near the AM/PM store, which was just beyond. As he opened his door, he asked, "Anyone hungry?"

Dillon shook his head.

Claire said, "No, thank you." Her sarcasm was evident.

"Coffee, Dillon? Claire?"

Dillon answered, "Sure."

"Black, Claire?"

Although still vexed, she said, "Maybe a little cream."

"Will you fill the tank, Dillon?" Max asked.

"I got it," Dillon responded.

"Don't even think about leaving, Claire," Max admonished.

Dillon finished pumping the gas and got back in the car. He turned in his seat to face her, hoping to soften the tension. He quietly asked, "How did you ever get fixed up with Casey Malone?"

She sighed, *why not?* And she told him the story of how she had practically been kidnapped from her work and then offered a job that paid more than she could even imagine. "I was in no position financially to say no."

Max returned, interrupting her story, and asked Dillon to please take the wheel. Dillon got out and thanked Max for the coffee. Max leaned in to give Claire her coffee along with a few snack bags. She watched them, stretching and sipping their coffees as they conferred outside. She supposed this would be dinner.

She considered trying to escape. There were other cars around. She could plead for help. Bad idea. She might get herself into worse trouble. She sat back in her seat and pouted.

Funny, how telling Dillon her story triggered the good memories. She sighed. What was she really running from? Maggie's kindness? Fabulous shopping trips? Little boutiques and expensive lunches? An elegant apartment she didn't have to pay for? The adrenaline rush when prospective clients signed on the dotted line? Truthfully, she loved the glamorous life she had lived for three years.

But still, there were rumors and that terrifying night. Maybe Casey didn't kill her co-worker. Then again... What business was Casey really involved in? And was Maggie a part of it?

She shuddered. Thankfully, Claire had saved most of her money. Getting far away was all she wanted now.

What about Bobby? What would he do when he found she wasn't at the cabin? Could he be the threat that Max thought he was?

Max interrupted her musings as he got into the passenger seat. "We will be turning back at the next roundabout. That should get us back to the City before nightfall."

Dillon asked Max, "You navigating?"

"I'll keep you on track. You and I can trade off driving. Right now, I need a little shut-eye. A little sleep might help you, too," he directed to Claire.

She didn't need much encouragement. She sat

back in her seat. Uncertainty and fatigue had caught up with her, and within two minutes after they were underway, she was sleeping soundly.

Claire shook herself awake from her nap when she felt the car slowing. It stopped in front of what appeared to be an old brownstone. Beside it, a garage door was opening. The car slowly entered, the door closing behind them.

Max led the way through a door that opened into a garden snuggled between the brownstones surrounding it.

A path, winding through beds of multicolored flowers, led to a large rock overflowing with trickling water, which pooled into descending smaller pools. The last of the glowing sunset reflected off the water, which ended in a pond filled with water lilies.

Max indicated the benches, an invitation to sit, as he disengaged the security system.

Claire took a deep breath and sank down on the one nearest the pond. She wondered where they could possibly be.

Just as the sun dipped below the horizon, she took in her surroundings. Admiring the many colorful flowers that surrounded her, she breathed in their delicious fragrance. This beautiful garden that bordered the pond with her favorite lilies was enchanting. "They are so beautiful!" she exclaimed, but then glanced at Dillon, somewhat embarrassed by her outburst.

Dillon smiled at the look on her face. "Amazing, isn't it?"

She nodded, remaining quiet.

Max stood facing them. "No one knows of this place."

"This is *your* place?" She wasn't sure why this surprised her.

"Only Dillon has been here. And before we go into the apartment, I want to emphasize that everything will be left exactly as we find it. Understood?"

"Of course." Her voice caught in surprise.

Max indicated they should follow him into the apartment. Max and Dillon entered.

Claire stopped in the doorway, taking in the minimalist room, decorated in varying shades of grays, whites, and black except for the multi-colored area rugs on the hardwood floors. The gray, overstuffed chair with two smaller, rust-colored swivel chairs facing it was inviting. An oblong marble table in between was an attractive accent.

Looking around her as she slowly came into the room, she noticed the freestanding fireplace on a tiled surface which backed into the corner tiled walls. A curved staircase, flanked by two tall silk plants that led to a loft which she supposed was a sleeping area, was on her left. When she looked up, she could see the shape of a desk on the opposing wall. Turning again, she saw a huge abstract painting on the wall with colors that complemented the furnishings in the room.

Max went behind the staircase to activate an electronic device, visible only when he touched it. With that done, he spoke, "We haven't actually gone into the City. We are somewhat isolated in this tiny community. I'm seldom here, so no one will expect to see anyone coming or going."

Max let them know he had some matters to attend to but invited them to make themselves comfortable. He suggested that Claire might like to walk in the garden as he and Dillon brought in food supplies from the car.

Claire was surprised but delighted to be able to

explore the beautiful garden with its water features and pools. She didn't know what to make of Max. How could he live in a space so lovely and still be... she didn't know what.

Later, she quizzed Dillon while Max was busy in the loft. "What is he all about?" she asked.

Dillon thought about what to tell her. "Well, he saved my life in Afghanistan—if that tells you anything." He saw that he had her attention. "I almost stepped on an IUD until Max ran and pushed me out of the way just in time."

Claire didn't say anything.

Dillon went on, "He would make a great attorney. I tried to find a way to get money to him for school without him knowing, but he found out and wouldn't accept it. He's an excellent Private Investigator, and we do well together—at least most of the time."

"Why do you say—most of the time?"

"Lately, we seem to get on each other's nerves a lot. It makes it difficult to work together."

Dillon smiled at Claire. "I think I'll see what we can rustle up for dinner." He headed for the kitchen.

When Max finally came down from the loft, Dillon cornered him: "Joining us for dinner? I have to tell you, there wasn't much to choose from."

"That's fine. I wasn't exactly expecting company," Max said.

Dillon looked at Claire, "How about you, Claire?"

"I'm not hungry. Sorry, Dillon."

"OK, then. Max? You have a plan? I didn't exactly expect to be here."

"I think it's Claire's turn to talk. After all, we don't know how clever her boyfriend—"

Claire cut him off, "Not boyfriend! Please!"

"Whatever. However clever this Romeo is, we need to be alert and ready." Max plunked himself down in the big chair and crossed his legs and arms as he waited for Claire.

His tone and manner irritated her so much she couldn't stop herself from challenging him: "How about—Who the hell are you two? Yeah, you were soldiers. But what about now? Why were you working for Casey? Maybe you still are! Why have you dragged me out here? What am I to you?" Her voice was cracking from anxiety. "I just wanted to get away!

Softly, Dillon asked, "From what—exactly? Yeah, I know, from Casey. But—?" He watched her as she finally moved to one of the swivel chairs and sat, twisting her hands, her head bowed.

Slightly less sarcastically, Max urged her on, "Come on, Claire. Spill the beans. It's only us."

She wondered whether he was smarting from her speech about not trusting them.

Max, taking in her forlorn look, softened his approach. "OK, Claire. What do you want to know about us?"

"Why are you a P.I. when Dillon is an attorney? It's obvious you are the one in charge."

"Money. Why else? Is there anything else you want to know?"

Claire could see that her question made him furious.

Maybe she should just tell her story—as much as she knew, anyway. She took a moment to calm down, then she cleared her throat. "When Nana died, my grandmother, I had no place to go. No money, just a job in a fancy restaurant. So Lucky and I moved in together as roommates."

Somewhat affronted, Dillon stopped her. "When

—back up—you lived with someone?"

"With Lucky."

Max asked, "Who is this Lucky?"

She shook her head. "Lucretia, my friend—everyone calls her Lucky. It's a better stage name, she says." Claire smiled as she pictured her: "I call her Happy-go-Lucky."

Dillon interposed, "Oh, of course! My client!"

Claire resumed, "That worked out fine for a while... until it didn't." She smiled sightly. "I vowed I'd never live with anyone ever again."

Max just stared at her. After a moment, he gestured for her to continue.

"When Bruno heard I was looking for a studio apartment, he began pressuring me to move in with him."

Dillon interrupted, eyebrows lifted, "And, who is Bruno?"

"Bruno, the owner of the restaurant. It was getting pretty intense—then Casey's goon came along—out of the blue. And Casey offered me this extraordinary opportunity. I can tell you that Bruno wasn't exactly thrilled when I quit."

Dillon probed, "Did Bruno threaten you?"

"Not in so many words. But I moved out of the

apartment so fast he didn't have a chance to do anything—and all that was thanks to Casey." Her voice had turned somewhat wistful.

Dillon interjected, "Do *you* think that Casey would put out a hit on you?"

"I don't know." She was near tears.

Max asked in a gentler tone, "What about your family? Your Mom? Dad?"

"I never knew my dad. Mom died when I was five. That's when I went to live with Nana. Somehow she always seemed to have enough money to take care of us—even to send me to a private school. But it was weird, when she died, there was nothing, not even her apartment."

Dillon was absorbing this information. "Stranger and stranger."

Claire attempted to pull herself together. Somewhat defensively, she said, "So, you see why I took Casey's offer. Anyway," she said somewhat proudly, "I have saved almost everything I made."

Max unfolded himself out of his chair. "You will need a new identity, which means new docs and all that," he mused. He noted how pale she was. She was totally exhausted. "Why don't we sort that out later? What we need now is rest."

No one disagreed. Max and Dillon took the loft, leaving Claire to sleep on the sofa.

She dozed on and off, the day's events running through her mind. Why did Casey want her dead? Did he know about the deposition? He hadn't even tried to find her. Should she have tried to talk to him about what she overheard?

Maggie had warned her to back off when she started asking questions about Casey's deals. But would she turn against her, too? They'd become close friends, or at least Claire had thought so. The idea hurt her, but she knew how much Casey trusted Maggie. They were so close.

The revelations about Casey hiring Dillon and Max really threw her. Whose side were they on? They seemed to think that Casey really was dangerous. How could they work for him if they thought that? Maybe they were dangerous too.

Hearing the little of Max's story he had divulged, she had uncertain feelings about Max. It was obvious that he was the one in charge, no matter Dillon's title. And when he wasn't mad at her, he was really very attractive. She thought it was his strength that attracted her—along with his piercing dark eyes. It was more than physical—but could she trust him?

Claire sat up and pulled her legs from the bed to the floor. They'd tried to convince her Bobby would betray her, but how did she know for sure that was true?

Embers from the fireplace still glowed, filling the room with warm light and shadow. She stood up quietly, listening for any waking sounds from above.

*Good*, she thought, *just snoring—one tenor, the other base*. That made her smile.

Her nap in the car had re-energized her. She walked softly to the kitchen to get a glass of water.

As she took a glass from the cupboard, she noticed sets of keys hanging beside the refrigerator. A plan began developing in her mind: What if she took the car, drove to Lucky's? No one would be looking for her there, surely—she could get her clothes and money. She always kept her passport in her bag with her. Then, she could take a cab to the airport. She'd leave the keys under the front mat and text Dillon where to find the car after she was high above the clouds on her way—away!

Hurriedly, she grabbed the car keys, found her jacket, and put on her shoes. She entered the garage, and very quietly opened the car door and slipped inside. She pushed on the garage door opener and started the car as the door opened. Before it was all the way up, she began to move the car forward, ready to take off as fast as she could, even without knowing in what direction to head.

Within a short distance, she had to stop for a traffic light. It gave her a chance to look around for something to guide her. She saw the dim glow of the City in the far distance. There should be an entrance onto the main highway nearby. She headed in that direction.

"Homeward Bound!"

As she drove, Claire found herself humming a tune she and Bobby had enjoyed together. Who were those two guys to tell her Bobby was no good? Just because he worked for Casey—well, she'd worked for Casey too. And so did they! They only guessed that Bobby was bad news. Maybe— just maybe—he was coming to save her!

That thought didn't sit so well, however. She didn't need saving or the obligations that might be expected. She just wanted to get to the airport, get on a plane, and find a safe place where she could just stop running and sort through all the chaos.

It was so late, the traffic was light. She should be able to get into the apartment without running into any neighbors. And then she would be on her way.

Max startled awake, not sure what he had heard. He quickly got up, and as he started down the stairs, he saw the empty couch. Pulling aside the blinds, he saw that it was still dark. He checked the kitchen and the bathroom—no Claire. He called up to Dillon, "Hey buddy, our guest has taken a runner." He opened the door to the garage—yep, no car. "Dillon, get down here."

"What!" Dillon groaned, pulling the covers over his head.

"Claire is gone!" yelled Max.

As the message penetrated through the fog in his head, Dillon threw back the covers and focused on what Max was saying. He got to his feet, leaning over the banister he called down, "What do you mean, she's gone?"

"What do you think I mean? She took the car and left."

Dillon quickly got into his clothes and almost ran down the stairs, "Why would she do that?"

"Pretty obvious, don't you think? She doesn't buy our story, and at the first chance, she took off."

"So, what do we do?"

Max just looked at Dillon. "We call Casey, of course."

# CHAPTER 11

Maggie stormed into Casey's office.

"Tell me you didn't!" she accused.

"What are you yelling about?" barked Casey.

Maggie marched over to the flat-screen TV on the wall behind Casey's desk and switched it on. The plaza shooting was the headline story. The reporter excitedly related that there were shots fired, one person critically wounded, but chaos was hindering the police investigation.

"Tell me you didn't try to get rid of Claire!" Her voice cracked, and her tears streamed. "They are showing surveillance footage before the shots." She thrust her finger toward the TV screen. "I saw Claire on it!"

"Why would you even think that?" His face showing his incredulity.

"Because you're afraid of what you think she knows, that when she ran off, she would head to the FBI!" She shook in her fury.

Casey stood. He put his hands on her shoulders and looked into her tear-filled eyes. "Maggie, I couldn't do that to Claire. You *know* me."

He turned back to the TV screen just in time to see an image of Claire running across the plaza. "I haven't heard anything from that useless lawyer! I don't know where she is."

Maggie, sniffing and wiping her tears, looked up at him. "She hasn't come to the office for a week! I've been to her apartment, knocked on her door, left countless messages on her phone. And when on the TV they said someone had been hit—and you had threatened to 'take care of her'..." She stopped, took a deep breath, and blurted, "I was afraid you'd decided to eliminate her!" She wailed.

"Oh, Maggie," his voice hurt and puzzled. He pulled her to him, holding her close as she struggled to regain control. "There are better ways to solve what may be a problem." He looked down at her as he pulled away. He lifted her chin gently and looked into her dark brown eyes, "Now, go find out what has happened, who was hurt, and everything you can. In the meantime, I'll locate Claire." He paused, then said, "I wish you had told me about this sooner." He turned away, then walked to his desk and sat. He retrieved a phone from the bottom drawer.

Maggie looked at him. "I'm sorry, Casey." She waited for his response.

Without looking at her, he waved her away as he punched in the numbers on the phone.

Sniffing, Maggie turned away and left the office, closing the door quietly behind her.

Casey was perturbed. Maggie really thought he'd have Claire killed. Well, that was one option if she really had betrayed him. But he didn't know that— not yet.

Where was that kid, Bobby? He'd sent for him hours ago. He should know... unless they had taken off *together*. Not a good thought. He didn't trust that young man's handsome looks or, for that matter, his attitude. Would Claire fall for that? When he heard they had been hanging out, he should have checked out that kid better.

He was interrupted by Maggie rushing in. "It wasn't Claire who got hurt! It was some man who was with her. He's now in the hospital in critical condition."

"That's a relief."

"There's more. The young man, Bobby, she was dating? We can't find him either. Maybe they're together!"

"I'm glad to see we are on the same page again," Casey smiled at her quizzically.

Maggie looked down, then stammered, "I shouldn't have accused you."

"No, no—it's OK. You were just afraid for her. You like her—huh?"

"Of course, she's Ruthie's kid!"

Casey said nothing in response to that. "Well, we still need to find her. She may be in trouble. We don't know who took that shot. Let's get to it."

Maggie nodded, took a deep breath, and headed out the door.

# CHAPTER 12

"Maggie. Maggie! Where in the hell? Mag—" Casey turned and then sputtered, "What are *you* doing here? Where is Maggie? She—"

"Relax, Casey. Maggie's fine. My guys made sure she got a coffee break." Sam smirked before he asked, "Isn't it *Claire* you should be asking about?"

Casey stood very still but said nothing. He took a deep breath and glared at Sam. He hadn't seen him face to face in years. Why was he smirking? Hard to tell; Sam was always the dandy. Dapper Sam was what everyone called him—behind his back. Never let you know what he was really thinking or feeling for that matter—everything an act.

Their last encounter had ended badly. Not even their neighborhood connection could overcome their mutual animosity. Sam's deep resentment; Casey's rage at Sam's attempt to manipulate him.

"What about Claire? What is she to you?" Casey growled, his fear for Claire's safety starting to surface.

"No, no. It's what she is to *you*! Your 'protege'— is that what it's called these days?" Sam chortled as he strode toward Casey.

*How could a human look so much like a hyena*? thought Casey. Then he began to realize that Sam didn't know the truth about Claire.

"We could have stayed friends, Casey. Partners! We could have been family!" Wheedling, "We grew up on the same streets. Buddies to the death was our motto. And then you actually moved the whole family away from the neighborhood. You couldn't even face me!" Sam's fury was mounting.

"I should have been cut in when you parlayed your real estate projects into a multi-billion dollar enterprise. But you refused to consider a partnership with *me!*"

Sam had begun pacing in front of Casey. Obviously, he had been sitting with the need for revenge in his gut for a long time.

"We shared territory! It would have been so

easy! And profitable! I could have taken over the whole protection scheme! The real estate front not enough for you?

"I was swindled out of what should have been shared! You had to take it all! You greedy bastard!"

Casey cut him off, thundering, "Sam! You know damn well we could never work together. Your tactics, my ways, could never mesh." He paused, lowering his voice, hoping to placate him, "Besides, Sam, all that was a long time ago…"

"No, Casey." He snarled, "It was yesterday. And yesterday, I got even. *Yesterday* was payback time."

"What are you saying, Sam?" Casey's voice was very measured, almost a whisper.

"Claire is gone, Casey." His voice filled with invective.

"That's crazy, Sam! What are you talking about? What do you mean, Gone?"

"On the news: one dead! My guy never misses! *She's dead.*"

A red flush had taken over Sam's face. His rage almost exploding.

*Had he tried to kill Claire! What if she was dead?* Casey was galvanized into action. He lunged for Sam. But before Casey could reach him, Sam reached for the holstered gun inside his jacket and shot Casey in the leg. At such short range, it was deliberately *not* a kill shot.

Casey fell to the floor, holding his leg in agony.

"That should stop you for a while!" Sam spit on him, then laughed, before striding out the door.

Maggie raced to get into the room, "Casey! I heard a gunshot—" When she saw him on the floor, she froze.

"I'm OK—just call 911 and get an ambulance here. Now!"

Casey was carefully lifted into the ambulance. The sirens blared, aggravating his mind, which was already in turmoil. *Where had all this begun?* As the pain meds started to take hold, he remembered...

The two couples, Casey and Maggie, Sam and Ruthie, headed for the boardwalk along the beachfront. The day had cooled down after one of those super hot summer days, and the light breeze from off the water was delicious. There were smiles, laughter at silly jokes, the boys doing their best to entertain their ladies.

On their way home, all that came to a sudden stop as a beat-up car came racing toward them. The four jumped off the path to avoid the crazy driver. He swerved at the last minute, just missing them. Hooting and yelling came from the car as it sped up down the road.

Sam was furious. Making wild declarations that he'd make them pay, he started to run after the car. Casey caught up to him and did his best to calm him down.

Ruthie stood frozen. She seemed to shrink into herself. As soon as they got to the apartment building, Ruthie scrambled up the stairs, throwing a "goodbye" over her shoulder as the door closed behind her.

Sam was taken aback. "Why is she acting like that?"

Casey shrugged aside Sam's question. As he took Maggie's arm, he told Sam he was walking Maggie to her apartment down the block.

Sam shrugged and took off down the street.

Once back, Casey hurried up the stairs to their apartment. He was upset with Sam and very worried about his sister, Ruthie, who was never that quiet and certainly not shy. He found her in her bedroom, crying, although she tried to hide it when he came in.

"Ruthie? Are you OK?"

"Sure, no problem." She gave him a teary smile as she scooted back on her bed.

"Talk to me."

She shook her head as she started sobbing.

"Hey, Ruthie. It's me—your big brother, remember? I swore I would always take care of you. But how can I if you don't tell me what's wrong?" He looked at her shaking shoulders, not knowing what to do.

There was a long silence before she, at last, quieted and looked up at him through her fingers. She grabbed a tissue from the table by her bed. Sniffing and blowing her nose, she tried to calm herself. She looked at the very uncomfortable Casey and gave him a timid smile. "Sit down, please."

He moved to her desk chair and sat, leaning forward toward her, his elbows on his knees.

"Casey, I know Sam is your best friend..." She paused.

"It's OK, Ruthie. Just tell me."

"Lately, Sam seems to be angry all the time. I glance at any guy, and he goes ballistic. Sometimes, he starts ranting—he hates 'this,' he hates 'that.' And if I disagree... he... he almost hits me! And then he gets mad because I run away from him! He scares me, Casey. He has a gun; his dad's—hidden in his closet—he showed it to me once.

"And tonight—when those stupid guys tried to scare us, I thought he was going to shoot them!" Her tears began flowing again. "I don't want to be his girlfriend anymore, but I'm afraid of what he might do if I tell him that!"

Casey moved to her and put his arms around her protectively. "Don't worry, Ruthie. I'll take care of it."

"But what if—"

"Shh. I said I'd take care of it." He smoldered. He would protect his sister, no matter the cost. "He won't ever hurt you or scare you again."

Casey left Ruthie and went downstairs onto the street, not sure what he *would* do. He hadn't realized Ruthie and Sam had gotten that serious. That had to stop. Now. Nobody put a hand on his sister, no matter how good a friend. Sam should know he'd crossed a line Casey couldn't ignore. That settled, at least for himself, he headed toward the neighborhood diner. He was famished.

A week later, Casey was drinking a beer as he watched a hockey game on TV. That got interrupted when he got up to answer the loud knocking on their apartment door. He opened it to find Sam standing there. "What are you doing here?"

"I came by to see Ruthie," Sam answered.

"You're kidding, right? You think you can man-handle my sister, and all you have to say is 'sorry' to make it all fine and dandy?" Casey's voice had gotten louder and louder as his anger grew.

"Look, Casey. I'd never hurt Ruthie—I want to make it right with her."

"Make it right? The only way you're going to make it right is to leave her alone. You don't talk to her; you don't go near her. Have I made it plain enough for you? Now go! Now!"

Casey slammed the door in Sam's face. He went into Ruthie's room to let her know everything was taken care of. She wouldn't have to speak to Sam, ever.

As he returned to his hockey game, he thought about his long friendship with Sam. Too bad it had to end that way, but family would always come first.

The sirens from the ambulance began to fade. Just before the pain medication took over and Casey dozed off, he thought, "If only it had been that simple."

# CHAPTER 13

After Bobby was sure Claire was nowhere around the cabin, he made a quick call to Sam. Sam had been very clear: find her; get rid of her.

Ordinarily, that order would be simple enough to follow. But she had gotten under Bobby's skin, more than a little.

Why had she left after she called him to come get her? He pulled out a cigarette as he sat on the front porch steps of the cabin.

Maybe he could convince her to just disappear—that's what she said she wanted on the phone, anyway. He could have her pretend to be dead, then take a picture of her 'dead'—job done! Sam would be happy. He'd found the perfect solution. That's how they do it on TV!

Of course, first, he had to figure out where she

went—and then convince her to pose so he could take the picture. Would he have to tell her that he was the one who had been hired to kill her? He'd figure that out later.

He finished his smoke, ground it out, stretched the kinks out of his neck and shoulders. Which way would she run?

# CHAPTER 14

"You can't go in!" the nurses told Maggie when she tried to enter Casey's hospital room. She should come back tomorrow during visiting hours. She argued until the doctor assured her that Casey was going to be fine; he just needed to rest after the surgery on his leg.

Maggie left the hospital, finally assured that he was in good hands. There was no point in going back to the office. What she really needed was to go home and sort out her jumbled feelings, worries and concerns.

She stopped by the stop-n-shop market to pick up dinner. She had no energy to cook. And yes, a bottle of Cabernet. Surely she deserved to let down for one night.

Her purchases made, she headed once again for

home. Home. Where was that exactly? Home once meant family, friends. All she really had left was Casey.

*And Sam!* She had been shocked when he stormed past her into Casey's office, and his two goons had marched her into the break room.

So many memories were stirred up. The fights— especially that *one* fight. Sam and Casey were always bickering, taunting each other. Their competition was fierce. She had gone out with Sam a few times. She chuckled at how irate Casey had been! Well, that was part of her motivation, wasn't it? For all the good it did. She had hoped it would make Casey jealous. Her shoulders slumped as she put her key in the lock.

Another key undid the deadbolt and arms full, she pushed her way in. Efficient as always, she put her takeout dinner in the microwave, uncorked the wine, and pulled a glass from the cupboard.

She discarded her coat, slipped off her shoes, and put them both in the hall closet. Before heading to the bedroom for her snuggly robe and slippers, dinner and wine were set next to her one comfortable, easy chair. She could finally settle and try to figure out what had happened between those two.

Her thoughts returned to that awful fight long ago between Sam and Casey. It was amazing they hadn't killed each other then.

Ruthie had pleaded with her to make Sam leave her alone, putting Maggie in the center of it all. She did her best. She emphatically told Sam that Ruthie was not going to see him again.

"You stay out of this, or else!" he had screamed, actually threatening her, scaring her, he was so angry. Still, Maggie had thought he would get over it—but maybe not.

She sat up and reached for the bottle to replenish her wine.

Getting comfy again, sipping her drink, Maggie reflected about when she had gone to work for Casey. It was scary at first, but he sent her to school, where she discovered she loved being able to learn! And he paid for all of it! So maybe it wasn't the romance she yearned for; he showed her in so many ways that he cared for her. She sighed and took another sip of her wine.

Maggie wondered, *could Sam carry a grudge after so many years? Yeah*, she thought, *Sam was known for his grudges, and he was violent when getting even.*

Suddenly, Maggie sat bolt upright and plunked down her empty glass.

Could *he* have put a hit on Claire to get even with Casey? Oh, my! She didn't want to imagine he would do something that vile.

Things were beginning to make sense. But how could she be sure? She had to know absolutely before she went to Casey with this.

# CHAPTER 15

Claire sighed with relief as she drove Max's car into Lucky's neighborhood. She even saw a parking place on the street just around the corner from the apartment.

She pulled in, locked the car, and started walking. As she turned the corner, she stopped abruptly.

What were those police cars doing in front of the apartment, their blue and red lights blinking, lighting up the street? Was someone hurt? She didn't see any ambulance or fire engine. She hoped fervently that Lucky was all right. What if Lucky had come back early from her audition?

Claire slowly walked toward the gathering of curious onlookers.

A young man in a hoodie moved away from the

group and turned toward Claire.

She gasped.

What was Bobby doing here? She had never told him where she was staying.

He quickened his step toward her. He put a finger to his lips as he approached, and then, taking her arm, urged her to go with him back around the corner, out of sight of the growing crowd.

"What's the deal, Bobby!" she exploded.

"Come on. Let's get out of here!"

"What are you doing here?" She questioned as she was being hurried along.

"Sam was here," he said gruffly.

"Sam?" Claire practically yelled, "Who is Sam?"

"Quiet down!" he urged and continued pulling her down the street. "We have to talk."

When they reached Max's car, she stopped him, showed him the keys, and opened up the car.

"OK. Let's talk," Claire snapped at him as she sat in the driver's seat.

"Not here—let's go to Mario's. We can talk there. And you'll be more comfortable if we're in a public place."

Claire looked at him, surprised. "OK. Thank

you."

She started the car. "So, tell me, where is this Mario's?"

Bobby had to practically drag Claire into Mario's. From the half-lit blinking neon sign to the dimly lit interior, to Claire it looked more like an after-hours bar than a restaurant. The sawdust on the floor for atmosphere and the smells of pizza from the kitchen didn't look inviting to Claire.

"What is this place, Bobby?"

"It's fine. I know these guys."

She reluctantly allowed herself to be ushered in. *Oh boy, what have I got myself into?*

"Come on. Nobody will look for us here," Bobby assured her.

Claire swallowed her apprehension and let him guide her to a corner table.

Once seated and impatiently twitching as he ordered a large pizza, she began, "OK, Bobby. What gives? How did you know where to find me? And what are all those cop cars doing in front of that apartment? I want to know—"

He stopped her in mid-stream. "OK, OK. Quiet down," he urged. "Just give me a chance, will ya?

Would you like a beer or wine?"

"I think coffee is a better idea," she countered.

"OK, sure. Coffee it is." He ordered a beer and a cup of coffee as soon as the pizza arrived.

Claire was surprised that she could have an appetite with all that was going on. Her first slice was gone before she realized she was snatching a second slice. She looked a bit embarrassed at Bobby. "This is the first meal I've had all day," she said.

Bobby looked relieved as he drank his beer and watched her eat.

"All right, Bobby. I'm fed, I'm awake," she said as she sipped her hot coffee. "Spill it."

He stopped in mid-bite, swallowed, and began, "Claire, you know I care about you."

She glanced at him with a raised eyebrow.

"I do!" he protested. "But before I met you, I got myself into a kind of a jam. I needed money. And I didn't even have a job. Then Casey took me on. He had heard I was from the neighborhood. It paid OK, but it wasn't enough." Bobby took a swig of his beer, wondering how to tell her the rest. "I owed some bad people a lot of dough. Especially Sam, who is a sworn enemy of Casey."

"So, what happened?"

"Sam's henchmen came after me. They said I had to fish over the money right then, or else." He shrugged his shoulders and drank more coffee.

"Or else what?" Claire demanded.

"Work for Sam."

She took in the shamed look on his face. His silence told her she wasn't going to like this.

"So you went to work for this Sam? Who knew you worked for Casey... and you were supposed to... Oh—OH!" she said as the realization hit her, "What? Spy on Casey?"

He nodded. "More than that. I was supposed to —" He glanced around to be sure no one was listening. "Take you out. Only I, uh, sort of missed you."

"Take me out?" She didn't understand. And then she did. Abruptly, she stood and started to leave.

"Hey!" He grabbed her before she could run. "You could say that I saved your life!"

She twisted away, and when he didn't let go, she slugged him on his jaw.

He didn't have time to duck. As he flinched, he released her.

"You tried to *kill* me!" Claire spat at him. She

was so enraged she didn't care who heard her. She ran out the door, got in the car and, tires screeching, drove off.

Tears streamed down her cheeks, making it tricky to drive, especially in the dark. She kept driving aimlessly as she tried to absorb what he told her.

Number one: it wasn't Casey! Number two—god, what did this Sam have against *her*? *Why take it out on me? It doesn't make sense.*

She'd paid little attention to where she was driving and wasn't sure where she was. She pulled over to the curb, the car idling as she began to reach for her phone in her bag. *Damn! Max threw it off the bridge!* Well, More important than where she was, where could she go?

Casey? But what if he had found out about her deposition? *Loyalty!* Would he—could he forgive her? He might be after her too. Did he know that she had overheard the threat to Henry?

*Maggie!* Would she understand? What if she were angry at her? Loyalty to Casey came first.

# CHAPTER 16

Rubbing his jaw, Bobby sat stunned, not sure what he should do. After a moment, he paid the bill, chugged down the last of his beer, and left the restaurant.

The police. *Geez,* he had to do something quick, or they'd mess up everything. He jogged back the few blocks they'd driven. He stopped at the corner of her street and took a furtive peek to see if the police were still in front of the apartment. He also was on the lookout for Sam's SUV. Neither seemed to be anywhere in the vicinity.

False alarm? That was what he had intended to tell the police. Sam would skin him alive if he knew or even suspected that Bobby had made the 911 call on him.

Bobby just hadn't been able to follow orders to

get rid of Claire. Why did Sam want to kill her? He hadn't given any thought to that when he got his first instructions to take her out and make sure it looked like it was Casey's hit. Bobby cursed.

What was he going to tell Casey? Bobby groaned. Maybe he was the one who had to disappear. It was all just too much.

Bobby wasn't sure where he should go. He couldn't figure out why Claire blamed him for— well, for shooting her—at her. *I mean, I apologized!*

He had heard through the grapevine that Casey was looking for him. *No way, Man!* So far, he had managed to stay out of his way. And Sam? What was he going to do about Sam? Maybe he should just leave town—for good. Forget Claire. That wasn't going to happen, anyway. Just had to face it.

\* \* \*

Claire was startled to find she had driven back to Lucky's neighborhood. She approached the street carefully. Thankful that no police or strange cars were around. Hardly believing her luck, she hurriedly parked in a space right in front of the apartment building. She slipped the car keys under the passenger side mat. Get in, get out was her immediate goal, and just hope the car wouldn't be towed.

Once inside the apartment, she stowed money and other essentials in her partially packed suitcase—she could buy later whatever she needed, like a cell phone.

As she took one more look around, the landline phone rang. It never rang! She noticed the blinking red light. There were messages. *Had to be for Lucky.*

She felt bad that she hadn't been able to let anyone know she was leaving. But it just wasn't safe.

She headed for the door, ignoring the ringing. Never mind, she muttered; she was gone. Long gone! The ringing stopped. *Finally.* Hail a cab and get out of here while she still could—to the airport.

# CHAPTER 17

Claire gathered up her things as the boarding call echoed throughout the terminal.

*All right! Aruba, here I come! Well, for a few days, anyway. And then? Maybe Costa Rica.* She smiled at the thought. *They say the people are really friendly, even if you don't speak Spanish.*

Once on the plane, she lifted her bag to the overhead, then took her seat next to the window. She began to breathe easier. For the first time in a while, she began to feel safe; safer anyway.

Her new phone vibrated. *Wow, they hooked me up fast!* The guy at the airport had promised immediate service as long as she used her old phone number.

By the time she tried to answer the call, it had already gone to voice mail. She pushed the voicemail icon. "Claire—leave—now! Get out as fast as you can!" *Bobby! Warning* her?

She listened: "I'm so sorry, Claire. Please just leave. I'll do what I can." It ended abruptly.

Her eyes filled. She felt the pounding of her heart. Anxiety and then anger did a war dance inside her.

Someone piled a bag in the overhead compartment, then sat, fiddling with the awkward seat belt. "Darn things never work right," muttered the older woman beside her. She glanced at Claire with a smile until she saw the state this young woman was in. "Can I help?" she asked tentatively.

Claire pulled herself together, shook her head, and explained, "I've just had some disturbing news. I'm fine, really." She turned again toward the window as the plane left the gate.

* * *

Aruba wasn't the tropical paradise the posters and video trailers suggested. Two days on the beach alone was about all Claire could handle. Maybe if she had a guy with her, she would feel different, but she didn't. And this place was designed with romantic couples in mind, not single ladies on the run.

Opportunities that were there for companionship weren't in any way attractive to Claire. She didn't appreciate the looks she got from the men or from their current companions.

Costa Rica—she had been reading about a place in the jungle with a nearby beach where all the turtles came every year to lay their eggs. That sure looked remote enough to keep her hidden. She could even pretend to be some kind of researcher. She'd figure that out later. Right now, she needed to make a reservation for that resort and reserve a plane ticket to San Juan.

\* \* \*

As the plane descended through the clouds, Claire marveled at all the green as far as she could see. Maybe Costa Rica was going to be her special place.

Claire retrieved her luggage and inquired about the shuttle that would take her to the riverboat. Once underway, she breathed deeply and realized how lucky she was to have the money she'd earned and saved. As a teenager, she'd been resentful that even though she had a part-time job, Nana insisted she save a percentage with each paycheck. The habit stayed with her, and she had continued saving even when working for Casey.

*Thank you, Nana, for all those lessons!*

The bus pulled up to a small dock where the riverboat awaited. She was excited: a new land, a new life! She climbed aboard and settled in, hoping to see jungle or even wild animals on the shore. As the boat got underway, however, all she saw was dilapidated warehouses and bodegas along the shore. Before disappointment could set in, the scenery changed. It became very green and lush. All signs of habitation disappeared. "Well," she said to herself, "I wanted remote!"

Two hours later, the boat docked at a rustic looking resort. Two strong men helped the passengers out of the boat onto land and then escorted them to the main building. She began to relax. Rustic looking, but not really rustic! Iguanas on the lawn looked fierce but moved too slowly to be menacing. Yes, she could relax here—and maybe even take that jungle hike they'd advertised.

\* \* \*

Claire sipped a wine cooler under the latticed overhang where the meals were served, relishing the moist air and gentle breeze on her skin. The flowers, which were even on trees, enchanted her with their brilliant colors and lush scents. The trumpeting sounds of the howler monkeys coming from the nearby rain forest gave her shivers until she was told how little these monkeys are. She'd learned to laugh at the slow-moving, reptilian looking iguanas that wandered onto the patio, and the little sloths as they did their tai chi moves along the tree branches. She enjoyed it all: walking the pristine beach, marveling at the sapphire blue ocean. She had wondered why she had to pull on high topped rubber boots to explore the rain forest, that was until her feet had sunk into the thick muddy paths that led through the jungle.

She even liked talking with the tourists. She didn't think of *herself* as a tourist, but as she watched even the older couples, she wistfully felt everything would be more fun with someone beside her, even just a friend, someone with whom to share these unique experiences.

Watching tourists arrive, then leave; new tourists taking the tours she had already taken, left her feeling empty, or at least—well, *restless!* Shouldn't she be happy? She was safe—or at least safer. She hadn't considered at all "what next?" At times, when thoughts of Bobby surfaced, she just got furious—or scared. He certainly wasn't what she wanted.

And then there were Max and Dillon. She realized it was really just Max, who filled her thoughts. Why Max?

She laughed at herself. Sure, aside from being good-looking, very strong, and that he always seemed to know what to do next. She sighed. Had she imagined the concerned looks he gave her?

She had run 3,000 miles away from her pursuers—whoever they were. She could sip wine coolers, relax in this balmy atmosphere, and all she could think about were her doubts and fears—and Max.

She admitted to herself she felt safer when she was with him. Were her feelings more than that? *Yes, he kept the truth about Casey from her.* But... Just the possibility created a warmth in her belly.

Where did he fit in? He confused her, first being distant and even dismissive, then wanting to help her with documents and the getaway. And taking her—well them—to his hideaway cabin, and even to his very amazing home, a sanctuary really.

She sighed, then closed her eyes, just letting the sounds of birds and the lush smell of the tropical flowers wash over her. What in the hell was she going to do?

# CHAPTER 18

Casey hobbled into his office on crutches shouting, "Maggie! Coffee! Where's the damn coffee?"

"Gee, Casey. I had no idea you'd be coming in. How are you feeling?" She was already making coffee at the wet bar in the back of the office. "How is your leg? Aren't you supposed to be home resting?"

"Ask me after coffee," he barked. He sat in the closest chair, which was in front of his desk. "Sorry."

"No problem, boss."

"Have you heard from Claire?" he asked.

She shook her head, then turned and brought him his coffee.

"If she was in trouble, she'd let me know," he

asked, "Wouldn't she?"

Maggie sat on the chair next to him. She had thought about this. "Casey... after the shooting in the plaza, she probably was so scared..."

"Of me?"

"Maybe. We still don't know why Claire disappeared." Maggie sat back in her chair and continued, "She is usually so bubbly." She smiled to herself. "She reminds me of Ruthie." She looked over at Casey. "You know how she is. She loves the work, the people, and certainly the perks." She took a sip of her coffee.

"So, what changed? Why did she run off?"

"Maybe Bobby?" she said. "That sharp kid from the neighborhood you hired? He really moved in on her. She was vulnerable, and I think he tried to take advantage of that—to get close to her."

"Yeah, a real good-looking guy. But would she fall for that?"

"I didn't like the effect he had on Claire. She was becoming secretive, even nervous. Even after I thought we had become friends."

"What are you saying, Maggie?"

"I don't trust him," she said vehemently, moving forward to the edge of her seat. "I think maybe he had something to do with her disappearing in the first place. I'm afraid she may not come back."

"What!" Casey yelled, trying to stand, but his leg gave way. He almost spilled his coffee.

Maggie leaped up to steady him. Once a mishap was averted, she spoke again.

"She's been gone almost a week." Her jaw tightened. "No word, no text, no phone call. I'm worried that something *did* happen to her. What if Sam *wasn't* lying?"

"Do what you have to do to track her down," Casey ordered. "What about those two guys? You know, the lawyer and the other one? Call them, get them in here. They may have some idea of what happened to her."

"Right on it!" Maggie said and quickly left her scowling boss.

# CHAPTER 19

Max and Dillon had taken Max's Porsche into the city, arguing as they drove. Dillon was not so sure about calling Casey. Max saw no other way to extricate themselves from the situation that they were in.

Dillon kept ruminating. "Where did she go? What spooked her? Why hadn't she talked to them?"

Max said, "It is obvious: she doesn't trust us—or anyone for that matter."

When they got to Dillon's office, he called Claire's apartment. Getting no answer—again—he threw down the phone in frustration.

Max remembered her old roommate. "Have you tried her friend, Lucky's number?"

Dillon dialed. Again, no answer. "What do we do

now?"

"What I said before: call Casey. We tell him we've been looking for her as he instructed."

"But what do we tell him about our search?" Dillon asked, then said, "Maybe we can *suggest* Bobby had something to do with it!"

Max responded, "Let's start with calling the airlines in case she actually got on a plane and took off."

"You think she'd do that?"

"That was her plan, remember? Just disappear."

"Yeah! OK. Let's get on that—checking the airlines," Dillon agreed. "This way, we've got something to report to Casey."

# CHAPTER 20

Max left Dillon and drove back to his place outside the City. He'd make his calls to contacts who could access whether Claire had boarded a plane and for where. Then he was finished. No more working with Dillon.

Max's frustration with Dillon had been growing. When Max said they should call Casey, he had barely responded. What was with him? Dillon seemed to drag his feet every time Max made a suggestion. But nothing substantive came from Dillon.

Max realized he hadn't been totally straight or open about his own plans. Why was he so hesitant about confiding in Dillon about his determination to get his law degree? He probably wouldn't understand how Max was driven to succeed on his own. He was fed up with rescuing Dillon from stupid decisions. This situation with Claire, as well as Dillon's dependence on Casey's money was more and more of an irritant.

Thank heaven he only had the bar exam to pass. Then he was done. The situation with Claire and Casey had stalled his progress, and the exam was coming up fast. He was still determined to pass it the first time.

Max arrived home, determined to take all the time he needed to study. He would put all other concerns aside. Surely he had done everything he could to help Claire.

Taking a break from studying, Max got up and poured himself a cup of coffee. He stood for a few minutes, looking out his kitchen window, admiring his flourishing garden, remembering how Claire had appreciated its special beauty. Why did that matter to him?

Max sighed. He had to finish this—whatever *this* was!—with Claire, and then with Casey. He knew that he personally was finished with Casey. With Claire? Not so sure. So, first, *find* Claire!

In the meantime, there was studying to be done.

He sat and booted up his laptop, accessing a trial exam to go over.

But Max was too conflicted to stay still for long. Should he stay with Dillon until all this was over and done? Maybe he should just have it out with him and see how it falls out. It had been boiling up inside him, and the tension was getting worse. He was sure Dillon felt it too.

Furthermore, Max had become less certain that Casey was the guilty party. Why would he put out a hit on his own 'special' employee? From what he had heard on the streets, murder didn't seem to be Casey's style. With his emphasis on protecting those close to him, how could he eliminate one of his own? And what was Bobby's involvement? Was he an instigator or just a pawn? It was a lot to sort out.

But all that aside, he had to get clear with Dillon, and then, hopefully with Claire.

Max saw that Dillon would never get through to her—on any level. Max sipped his coffee. Was he, in spite of himself, attracted to her? Oh, yes. But was she trustworthy? Maybe. Maybe not. She had worked for Casey—as his protege? What did that even mean? Somehow, he knew he had to know a lot more about her. He went back to the sample test.

A thought intruded: Couldn't he justify writing her off as an unsolvable case? He sighed. That just wasn't who he was.

Once Dillon was out of the picture, Max would track her down on his own. Soon his connections would help him find her plane departure. Then he would decide if Casey was a threat—and whether he would reveal to him Claire's whereabouts.

# CHAPTER 21

Two days later, Max stormed into Dillon's brand new office in Casey's building. "What the hell do you think you're doing, going to Casey without me?"

Dillon startled. "Hey, hold on! You were the one who said we should talk to Casey."

"It might be a good idea if we agreed on *what* we would tell him. I just got a call, ordering me to find Claire *now*, and bring her home. What did you tell him?"

"Look, I know you're skeptical about Casey, but —"

"What did you tell him?"

"That we should have a good idea of her location really soon."

"Grand! You have a plan for that, Dillon?"

"I don't think Casey did the deed. I think he is really worried about Claire. We should find her."

"We. You mean *me—which is fine*. I will find her, and then *I* will decide what happens next. Have you considered that Casey might want to find her to shut her up! This is it, Dillon—no more. No more cases; no more calling me to bail you out. I'm done. I have plans of my own, and they do not include you."

Dillon's jaw dropped as he watched Max storm out.

Max charged into the elevator and slammed the down button. That was not how he had wanted that to go! He realized he had to get a hold of himself. Man! He had lost it.

He exited the building. As his breathing returned to normal, it occurred to him that maybe it was for the best. Dillon wanted to settle; he did not. And now nothing was stopping him from finding Claire, and then... time would tell.

# CHAPTER 22

Max wasted no time. His P.I. contacts didn't take long to locate Claire's flights, first to Aruba and then to Costa Rica. And although he immediately set out in pursuit, he questioned himself: *What is so urgent about my finding Claire? Pride? Attraction?*

He hadn't even figured out how to approach her or how to persuade her to return with him. Should he convince her that Casey was not trying to hurt her? Did he believe it? *Why am I really going after her?* It was all heavy on his mind.

Why Costa Rica, he wondered. As the sound of the plane's drone lulled him, he couldn't keep his thoughts away from Claire. Who was she really? A brash, angry bitch, or a scared little kid who wanted to run and hide. She was feisty, for sure!

And she had been through a lot. Whether the shot had been aimed at her or not, it had been traumatic. He was grateful that Frank had pulled through. He needed to tell her that. She didn't need to carry that guilt around.

And maybe he should modify his own approach. His actions up until now had certainly not been effective. Had he scared her off? Maybe that old saying, you catch more flies with honey than with vinegar, was true.

He smiled. She was no fly, but she sure had been running away. If she really intended to keep running, she had to get a fake ID and documents that would keep her hidden.

As the plane began to descend, he hoped he could persuade her to return with him. Maybe she had mellowed a bit in the tropics. He certainly hoped so!

# CHAPTER 23

Feeling restless, Claire decided to take her daily walk to the dock at the river's edge, where the tourists disembarked. Why not? She enjoyed being a friendly face to greet them.

She was just in time to see the first visitors climb onto the dock. As the last passengers were helped onto the dock, she gasped. "That couldn't be!" she said aloud as she watched Max making his way out of the boat.

As he waited for his luggage to be off-loaded, he took in his surroundings. And he saw her. Different! No longer the businesswoman. The pale yellow sundress and sandals, and her hair loosely touching her shoulders as the gentle breeze tossed it, was very appealing. Then, he registered the incredulous look flooding Claire's face.

"What are you doing here?" She sounded more than surprised, even afraid.

Max halted his steps toward her. Claire seemed frightened—of him. He watched as she took small steps backward away from him until she became aware that she had no place to hide.

He hid his hurt at her reaction. Gently, he said, "Maybe we could have dinner together." He paused, hoping for a positive response. "I'm here to help. It's time to stop running, Claire."

Tears filled her eyes. It was his tone, not the words. "Well," she said as she gazed at him, "I'd probably need a boat to do that." *Why couldn't she think of something clever to say?*

Max smiled, indicating the group heading for the main lodge. "I better sign in." He asked, "How does six o'clock sound?"

The departing group was disappearing into the lodge. He picked up his duffel and started off without waiting for an answer. "See you at dinner," he called back to her.

She was shocked; she couldn't move. Her mind tried to absorb what had just happened. *Stop running? Is that what he said? What was the matter with him? Didn't she have very good reasons to do just that?* Her feet finally were able to move. She started walking slowly without direction until seeing a bench that faced the rain forest just beyond. She sat down, troubled. Everything was hidden, even frightening unless one had a guide.

*Was Dillon coming next? Why? I paid them; wasn't it over for them? Unless he was Casey's henchman. But... Max seemed so—different! What was his angle? Why was he being so—nice?* Getting up from the bench, she walked to her room.

*Why? Why is he here? What does he want? Was it a trick?* Once inside, she started pacing back and forth in her small room, arms crossed, hugging herself.

"I paid them!" she exclaimed aloud to no one. She stopped in front of the mirror hanging above the dresser. Looking at the image facing her, she spoke again, "What am I doing here? Who *am* I?" Now her tears began flowing; she plopped on the edge of the bed and let the tears become sobs.

She was so confused. *Where was there to run? And what then?* She let herself fall back on the bed. Pulling a blanket over her, she curled into a fetal position, snuggled in the comforter, and fell asleep.

# CHAPTER 24

Max unpacked his duffel and then took a long hot shower, letting the heat unlock the tension in his back and shoulders. Although the water soothed his apprehension, he still asked himself, "What do I think I can do here?"

He seldom let a client get under his skin as he had Claire. He'd done everything he could for her —even inviting her (well, maybe not inviting) to his sanctuary. And then she took off! No explanation, no reason! *But she wasn't just a client, was she?*

He turned off the shower, dried, and then wrapped the towel around his waist. He lay on the bed, trying to puzzle out the situation. But the sweet vision of her waiting on the shore kept intruding until he fell asleep.

When Max awoke, he was startled to see how dark it had become. He turned on the bedside lamp and quickly dressed. He headed toward the outdoor dining area he had been shown when he arrived. He wondered if she would be there. He didn't want to miss her. He had no idea of the time —he'd left his watch behind in his hurry.

Max looked around to see if Claire was there. A few couples were still dining, but no Claire. As he drew in a deep breath, a waitress approached him, indicating an empty table which he took. May as well, he thought.

He had little appetite. He was anxious about Claire. She was obviously surprised to see him here—even shocked. Well, good. Maybe he could get some honest answers to his questions. He reached for his glass of water.

And there she was!

Max stood, letting her find him. In the soft light, she looked very beautiful—and vulnerable. She had pulled her hair back into a ponytail. Her light frock was so different from her usual working attire. The effect was transformative.

As she came toward him, he said, "You look

lovely this evening," Before she sat, he noticed how little makeup she wore, and how swollen were her eyes. *Did I cause that?* As she sat, he asked, "Would you like some wine?" She nodded. "Red or white?" he asked.

Claire shrugged her indifference, not meeting his questioning eyes. He told the waitress to bring them each a glass of white wine as well as a soup that would go well with the wine.

"Claire," he waited for a response. Finally, she looked up at him. "I'm not here to hurt you," his voice was warm.

"Why *are* you here?" timidly, she asked. Then in a stronger voice, she questioned, "Did Casey send you?"

"No—well, he thinks he did—but no. That's not why I came here. And before saying anything else, I don't think it was Casey who tried to have you killed."

She nodded. "It was Bobby who tried to shoot me. He told me that someone had hired him. A *Sam,* I think. But I don't know why!"

"So, you know it wasn't Casey."

"I don't *know* anything! I don't know who or what to believe." After a moment, she added,

"Maybe Bobby was lying. Maybe Sam *and* Casey both want me dead!"

Max reached for her hand. "Dillon believes it was someone trying to hurt Casey by hurting you."

Removing her hand from his, she sat up straighter. "It wasn't Casey? Really?" Her tears once again flowed, but this time it was a mixture of relief, surprise, and even hope.

"Apparently, Casey is worried about you. It seems genuine."

"It really wasn't Casey?"

"It seems our assumptions were the result of a lack of reliable information. We can get into all that later," Max said. "But I—"

They were interrupted by the waiter, who asked if the gentleman would like to order anything more.

Max smiled at Claire as he said, "Let's enjoy the evening." And to the waiter, he said, "We'll also need a couple of menus."

Claire was about to protest, but acquiesced when Max urged, "Please."

Max attempted conversation to put her at ease. "Have you been on any of the jungle tours?" he asked.

Claire cleared her throat before answering, "I have. You have to put on these high boots before the tour guide will take you hiking. I thought it was dumb until I almost sank into the mud halfway up my calf." She laughed at herself, not sure why she was telling this story.

Max smiled appreciatively at the effort she was making. He asked, "Have you seen any wild animals since you've come?"

"The iguanas are probably the most 'wild'. I would love to see a jaguar—at a distance. But that's not too likely."

The waiter returned with two wine glasses and the bottle of white wine Max had indicated. "Maybe just tapas for now," Max instructed.

As Max poured the wine, he could see that Claire was still uncomfortable. He filled her glass and raised his own in a toast. "To new beginnings—for each of us." He was happy to see she took a sip. He felt intensely drawn to her, and couldn't stop himself from saying,

"This setting suits you." He watched surprise fill her eyes. "A beautiful place for a beautiful woman," he offered, hoping for a sign of encouragement.

Claire stood abruptly. She seemed distraught.

Max stood immediately, reaching for her hand.

"No, please—I need to think," she said.

Impulsively, he took her hand and drew her to him. He then pulled her into his arms and held her close. She didn't pull away. He felt her breath begin to accelerate. He looked into her eyes, watching her carefully. He then took her face into his hands and kissed her—at first gently and then deeply.

Before she could escape his embrace, he released her, but he kept her hands in both of his. He raised her hands to his lips and kissed them. "Good night, Claire. Sleep well." He turned and walked away.

Claire was hugely confused, angry at herself. *Why did I let him kiss me?* And at the same time, she acknowledged how his kisses ignited a fire in her. She was frustrated with her conflicting emotions. She started walking slowly away from the empty dining area, muttering to herself, "I am in such trouble."

# CHAPTER 25

Max chose to walk calmly to his cabin, although he did not, in the least, feel calm. *What possessed me?* He was as surprised by the kiss as Claire evidently was. *Still, she hadn't resisted. She returned my kisses.* He quickly entered his quarters, more confused than ever.

What now? He may have ruined any plan he'd made to get her to stop running and return with him to the City. And what *were* his intentions? No good could come from getting involved. However, he wasn't blind to the fact that everything had already changed.

Could they just go back to how it was before as if nothing had happened? Yes! It had to be that way.

He shed his dinner jacket and shirt along with the rest of his clothes. He grabbed his robe.

Retrieving a cold bottle of water from the mini-fridge, he sat on the bed, letting his head rest against the headboard.

He knew he kept people, especially women, at arm's length. Growing up through the foster system had taught him well: don't let anyone get too close—and never try to get close; you will always be hurt. People lie; they cannot be trusted—they will always bail, no matter what promises are made.

As he sat in the nearly dark room, sipping his bottle of water, the image of his 5$^{th}$ grade teacher, Mrs. Sloan, surfaced, bringing with it, hurtful memories.

She had made him believe he could become something. No one before had ever encouraged him like that. But it was just a lot of words! She left, just disappeared from the school. He didn't know why. She never said anything; She was just gone; the first of too many.

Max shook his head and sighed. Tonight was stirring up a lot of buried memories, all of which taught the lesson: don't trust anyone and never get involved... especially if it's a beautiful woman!

Even his friendship with Dillon...

Following high school, Max had enlisted in the army. That began his association and then friendship with Dillon. Both were in line for their physicals. Dillon made a crack that Max wouldn't have any problem passing a physical—and it was true.

Max had worked out ever since he had been bullied in middle school. That ended when he gained his 6'3" height. The tables turned quickly, but he continued with weights and running—this time for the sheer sense of freedom it gave him. The track team coach in high school saw him and tried to recruit him for the team. He turned him down. He ran for himself only—not for, and definitely not from, anyone. *Is that what he sensed from Claire? That she was on the run from her problems?*

Meeting Dillon in the way he did somehow made it OK to get to know him. He and Dillon were nothing alike. They were as different as black and white in every way. Dillon admired him! And to him, their diverse backgrounds seemed irrelevant. A true bond was forged when they were on patrol together. Max saw and identified the IUD in the road just as Dillon was heading toward it. He had roughly pushed Dillon aside from a close, lethal step. Dillon never forgot it.

This memory made Max uneasy. He rose off the bed and went outside. The jungle sounds filled the air, and the thick vegetation from along the river filled his nostrils. He breathed it all in. It was humid, but not unpleasant. He wished he hadn't stopped smoking! He sure could use a cigarette.

He leaned against one of the posts that supported the overhang. He had to square things with Dillon, let him know why he was leaving. He probably wouldn't get how important sitting for the bar was to Max. All that had been so easy for Dillon. But that was OK. He knew why, and he needed no one's approval or even understanding.

# CHAPTER 26

The morning sun streamed through the window of her rustic cabin onto Claire's closed eyes. She stretched and gradually opened her eyes. It was much later than when she usually awoke. "I'm going to the beach," she declared.

She quickly left her bed and scrambled for her bikini and the sea-blue beach wrap she had bought at the gift shop.

She skipped breakfast. It was probably too late, anyway. She had no appetite, and she certainly wasn't ready to face anyone—*him*. She walked until finding the entrance onto the empty beach. No one was around, not even the famous turtles. She smiled: *All mine—for this morning, anyway.*

The surf appeared a bit rough—she sighed. *Better not try swimming alone in that.* She sat down on a sand dune and let herself relax into the rhythm of the waves pounding on the shore. She loved the salty tang of the air here. She sat hugging her knees, trying not to think. If she could just leave the old memories behind, hold on to the peace she felt here.

A voice broke her reverie. She glanced behind her—yes, it was him. She said nothing; she had nothing to say.

"I didn't mean to startle you," Max said.

"You didn't." She continued to gaze out at the blue-green waves coming ashore.

He sat down next to her, keeping the silence between them. This was a first, he thought as he ran the sand through his fingers. No anger, no recriminations or outbursts—not even tears. Something definitely had changed.

Claire finally broke the silence. "Why did you kiss me?" she asked in what sounded like a simple question.

Max gave no answer, but he turned his head to look at her. She deserved an answer, but he didn't have one to give her, at least not an honest one. Finally, he said, "I felt... it just happened."

"No apology?" Claire raised an eyebrow.

"Do you need one?"

She shrugged her shoulders. Looking down, not at him. She said, "No, I guess not." She glanced at him and then stood up, brushing the sand off her legs. She started walking toward the water.

He followed her. "Claire?"

She turned to face him.

"We need to talk—honestly with each other."

She stood very straight and said, "It's about time!" But then looking at the exasperation appearing on his face, she exclaimed, "No! I don't mean it that way!

"We *do* need to talk. It's just... I'm scared. I don't know what you want from me. I don't know why Bobby—or Sam would want to kill me. If you found me this quickly, when does everyone else arrive?" Seeming to rush to get her words out, she pleaded, "Why are you so concerned about me? Why should I trust you?"

Max reached toward her...

"No, please don't," she said, taking a step back away from him. He saw tears threaten as she quickly wiped her face and began walking away.

"Claire!"

She stopped.

"I understand; I do. Why should you trust me? All I can say is..." He raised his arms to her. "I would *never* cause you harm."

Claire shook her head and turned to go.

"I know that is not enough. But I believe we can sort everything out if we give each other that chance." He paused, waiting for her response. "Can we just talk?"

She faced him, trying to determine whether he meant what he said. "OK—just talk." She turned away again, throwing over her shoulder, "I need to change. I'll come to your cabin when I'm ready." She stopped and turned once again. "And we can find a private place—to *talk!*"

Max nodded his agreement. Frustrated, knowing she might run again, he said, "I'll be there." And with a hopeful look at her, he walked away, leaving her standing on the dune.

# CHAPTER 27

Claire knocked on Max's cabin door. Smiling with relief, he immediately opened it and invited her in.

She gave him an *oh-no-you-don't* look and quickly turned around and started walking away.

Max realized he had mis-stepped—again, "Hold on, Claire!" He called after her. "Look, I was only being polite. I wasn't assuming anything."

"Sure," she said.

When he caught up with her, he matched her pace, letting her take the lead.

Claire stopped. And feeling a little silly, she said, "I don't know where I'm going."

"Well, neither do I," he replied. "So, let's find a place together."

She gave him a careful look but nodded. Max

simply started walking.

A short distance away, they came to a bench set apart from the main compound.

Without either one saying anything, they both sat. Max waited for as long as it took for her to calm down, and hopefully, open up.

Claire tried to slow her breathing. She knew they had to talk, but she didn't know how to begin or what to say. How much should she believe anything he had to say?

"I want to know—" What did she want to know? Her thoughts were jumbled, leaving her uncertain and confused.

"I imagine you want to know you can trust me," Max said. "If we can get that part out of the way, maybe we can work together to figure everything out." He waited for some sign from her that she heard him.

Claire very much wanted, needed, to trust him. And what choices did she have? There really was no place to run—not with her own name on her passport and credit cards. *Why hadn't she thought about that before running?* She had felt trapped when all she wanted was to feel safe!

She glanced over at him and saw he was waiting for her to make some kind of decision. Taking a deep breath, she finally spoke, "You were right. I ran. I always run when I'm scared or don't want to face something. I can't help it."

He responded with a slight smile which put her somewhat at ease. "Why do you think that is?"

Claire took another deep breath before she continued, "As a kid, Nana kept a tight leash on me. You know, stay home, no friends here, no sleepovers. 'It's too dangerous' was her automatic response to anything I wanted to do. No other explanation. One day, I guess I was about thirteen, I got irritated with my friend who I usually walked home with. I took off on my own, full of confidence I could take care of myself. But—" She stopped.

"What happened, Claire?"

"Two boys were walking behind me. It felt like they were following me. I started to panic; I walked faster. They came just as fast, and then they started hooting and laughing, yelling stupid words at me. I tried to ignore them until I saw a car was slowly coming up the street and was almost beside me. I started running, those guys *were* after me! Just before I got to my apartment building, two tough-looking men came out of a nearby doorway and confronted the boys as I ran into my place. The boys and the car took off in a hurry." Her breathing had become shallow as she told her story. Finally, she went on, "I knew a girl who got attacked on her way home from school; she was thrown into a car and was never heard from again. I don't know what would have happened if those men hadn't shown up."

"I see," he said quietly. Her story resonated within him. He understood fear.

"I grew up in the foster system," Max began. "It was a good thing I could run fast before I finally grew taller than the bullies who tried to make my life miserable. I trusted no one. Grown-ups made promises that were never kept, and more often than not, they were more vicious than the bullies at school."

Claire asked, "How did you..."

"Escape? By trusting no one... that is until I met Dillon. Actually, he insisted on getting to know *me*." Max laughed at the memory of their first meeting. He told her how they met, and the time in Afghanistan when Dillon almost stepped on an IUD. He omitted his part in saving Dillon's life.

"Anyway, we became almost like brothers."

"And now?"

Max looked at her. "You don't need to worry about Dillon showing up here. I told him that I would handle this mission."

"You made me so angry when you said I have to stop running as if I had a choice! But you were right. That is what I've been doing. I just don't know how to stop." She wiped away the few tears that had escaped her eyes.

"Please don't run from me anymore, Claire. Let me help." He tentatively smoothed away a lock of hair that had escaped her ponytail. "OK?"

"OK," she sighed. "So, what do you need from me?"

"Will you tell me—what is your relationship with Casey?" he asked, filled with uncertainty about what she would say.

"I hardly ever talk to him. Maggie is really my boss—and I thought, my friend." Tears threatened her again. "She knew my mother when they were little girls, best friends." A smile lightened her teary eyes.

Max's relief was evident from his expression.

"Nana never talked about my mother—too

painful, I guess. But Maggie made me see my mother, what she liked, what she hated. Maggie said my mom never told her who my dad was. I never found out. Anyway, Casey always looked out for Ruthie and Maggie. He protected them. Maggie said he almost went mad when she was killed."

"Went mad?" he queried.

"Maybe she said he got mad—anyway he tried to go after the gang that did it. Maggie says that family and the neighborhood are what matter to Casey." She straightened up with a new thought: "I don't know what I am to him, but I guess it doesn't make sense that he wants me dead." She sounded hopeful. "And I don't know for sure that he had Henry—my colleague—killed. But *someone* did," Claire said, her fingers rubbing her forehead in frustration.

"He never talked to you about any of this?"

"Casey never talked to me at all! Everything I know came from Maggie." She slumped against the back of the bench. "But what if he found out about my making the deposition? Nothing else makes any sense." Her voice had turned a little wistful. "Bobby's claim that someone named Sam hired him—makes even less sense. I think he was just trying to be a big shot. Casey *must* be behind the shooting."

"I don't think he was. He wanted Dillon and me to find you—he seemed genuinely concerned about your welfare, Claire. I don't think Casey is the guilty party here."

"But Bobby works for him. He actually admitted trying to shoot me and then acted like he missed me on purpose! Instead, he got poor Frank."

"You should know that Frank pulled through. He is going to be fine."

"Oh! I am so relieved."

"What if Bobby was *really* working for *Sam*?" Max asked.

"Who is this Sam? I was so shocked when Bobby told me he had shot at me, I didn't really ask who Sam was. And why would this Sam want to kill me? I don't know him at all! Why target me?"

"I don't know the whole story yet. But I intend to find out." He stood, helping Claire to her feet. "Come on. I want to check something out at the lodge—and we can get some food at the same time. You skipped dinner and breakfast, remember?"

After ordering a light lunch, Max showed her the brochure he had obtained from the bell captain. "We need to leave here as soon as possible," Max said. "We may have unwelcome visitors if it *is* Sam who's determined to get rid of you. There's a small plane a short distance from here that ferries passengers in and out of San Juan. There we can get a plane to the States."

"A plane to where?" she asked, both puzzled and concerned.

"We both need to see Casey," he urged.

Claire sat uncomfortably with this idea for a few moments. Then she straightened up. "I'm confused. You are leaving Dillon out of this." She was interrupted by the waitress bringing their lunch.

"Ah. That." Max sat back in his chair. He took a moment before he confessed, "Dillon and I are no longer working together."

"What?" She almost dropped her fork in surprise. "What happened to 'almost like brothers'? Is he behind my attack too?"

"No, no," he reassured her. "It was personal. Even brothers have to go their own ways sometimes."

"Oh," she frowned, waiting for a further explanation, until she realized none was coming. She took a few bites of her salad to fill the silence.

Max put his fork down. "Right now, we should finish here; then make our plane reservations and pack."

She hesitated, still deciding whether to follow his lead. "You really think we should confront Casey?"

"Not confront. Talk to him. Just talk. By his reaction, we'll know if he wants you dead or not." He took her hands and helped her rise. "You... We... Can't run and hide forever. We have to get to the bottom of this—and do it before everything blows up—including us."

She warmed at his touch, and although knowing it was illogical to feel so safe with him, she acquiesced as he pulled her in the direction of the lodge.

# CHAPTER 28

The plane was small, old, and too noisy to even attempt a conversation. *Lots of time for thinking*, Claire thought; *maybe too much time!*

They settled in for the short flight, hoping to get to San Juan in time to catch their plane for the States—any state! Luckily, the plane for JFK in NYC was delayed, and they easily got their luggage as well as themselves on board.

Once buckled in, Claire asked the question that had been plaguing her, "So... What happened with Dillon? I thought you two were partners."

Max looked out his window, took a breath, and turned toward her. How was he going to explain? "Let's just say we've decided to go our separate ways."

"That won't do, Max. I need to know. Whether you like it or not, I am involved. Please—you want me to trust you. You have to start by trusting me." The last sentence was spoken softly, a small smile emerging.

He was quiet for some time.

Claire urged him once more, "Max, please?"

"This wasn't a sudden decision. Before you hired us, I was going to pull back from the work I did for Dillon."

"You weren't partners? You seemed so close."

"Well, yes, we do work well together. It's hard to explain." He checked outside the window again.

"Please try, Max."

"I've wanted more—to be more than a P.I. for some time. Dillon's heart really isn't into law. He does what he has to, but—"

"But what? You began to have reservations?"

"I wanted corroboration on some of the decisions he made. I wanted... I want to be my own expert... not need him for that."

"Couldn't you just tell him that?"

"Not exactly."

"What do you mean?"

"I've been going to law school in my time off—

which was put off longer and longer as he kept taking jobs without consulting me. The final straw was when he insisted we hook up with Casey."

"You mean me," she said, trying to better understand.

"Yes—well, actually, just before you. That was the latest example." His words could be taken as a slap, but his voice held a different quality, a caring? "Look," he said. "I was scheduled to take the bar exam, and I needed to study hard if I wanted to pass it the first time. I was determined to do just that. But—"

"But, I entered the picture." She thought for a moment. And then the realization hit her: "You weren't really angry with me. Frustrated?"

"Exactly! And annoyed. Casey hired us to find you. But frankly, I didn't take your situation that seriously—even after the shooting."

"Yeah! At ME!" she exclaimed slightly incredulous, her loud voice attracting the attention of other passengers.

"I thought it more likely a random shooting," he softly placated her. "However, when Casey came up as a likely suspect—everything changed."

"How so?"

"I couldn't just walk away."

"Why?"

He paused again, considering his words. It wasn't so much the situation he couldn't explain. It was his feelings, and he wasn't quite ready to expose them to her.

"Whatever you think of me, Claire, I am a man of my word. You were in trouble, and we'd agreed to help. I was afraid Dillon might have trouble putting you first. A conflict of interest might be the best way to say it."

"Between me and—?"

"Casey Malone."

Claire leaned back in her seat and sat with the implications of what he was telling her. "And now?" she finally asked.

"It's complicated. *I* complicated it. I blew up at Dillon just before I tracked you down in Costa Rica."

"So, it's really only you—" she didn't complete the sentence. She tried to put everything together, but her heart had begun beating faster— uncertainty? Fear? Where did she fit in this puzzle? Her thoughts were jumbled. *So who is Max really working for? Casey? Me? His kisses?*

*NOT HELPFUL!* Those thoughts just drove her toward trusting him. She knew it was her desire for him that had kept her awake last night. She gave herself an internal shake. *Get it together!* she admonished herself.

Taking a deep breath, Claire asked, "Why did *you* come after me?" She congratulated herself on being able to get those words out. But how did she want him to answer?

"It was clear to me that you were panicking and running without a clear plan—and I was afraid you were running from us—from me." He waited for her response.

"I guess I was, in a sense, running from you both. I was so scared. But I really didn't think anyone would bother coming after me if I just got out of the country. And I did pay you—well, Dillon. *Did* he pay you?" Her voice concerned.

"That wasn't my issue. Someone shot at you. And you needed help that I could give, and—"

Claire interrupted him, asking, "*Could* give?"

"Wanted to give." Max reached for her hand, holding it until she gently withdrew it.

She wanted so much to hold on to him but feared her growing feelings for him.

Happily, the flight attendant interrupted the awkward moment, bringing their dinner trays. Claire had forgotten that they still fed you on international flights. She had little appetite, her stomach tight from the direction of their discussion. She was grateful for the reprieve.

Max also seemed to relax a bit as the tray was placed on his let-down table. They both needed a time-out.

As she picked at her food, she tried to untangle all the strings of their conversation. *Huh! Some conversation. More like pulling teeth.* She tried to focus on 'what next?' They were soon landing in New York. Why was he so certain she had to talk to Casey? Talk! Who just *talked* to Casey? She would be lucky to get a word in edge wise.

Just untangling the piece of the puzzle concerning Casey was no easy task. She felt herself becoming warm as the implications started to emerge. Yes! She certainly did have to talk to Casey! And this time, she would get answers: Why had he really hired her three years ago? What was his relationship to her mother? And who killed Henry, her obnoxious colleague?

The plane had descended without her noticing until a forceful bump indicated they had landed. For the first time, she felt ready to move forward, instead of running. *No more running!*

As Claire gathered her things, Max texted Dillon: *I have Claire. Plane at JFK just landing. On our way to Casey.*

She looked at Max, "Who were you contacting?"

"Doesn't matter."

"And you want me to trust you!"

"Dillon! I texted Dillon."

"Why?"

"I have to get straight with him. Besides, we—you and I—want to handle our conference with Casey—"

She interrupted, "No, not you and me. Just me. I will talk to Casey—by myself. I don't need a watchdog."

"Claire, that's not how it is—" His annoyance showed, "Not what I am."

"I don't need you or anyone watching over me." With that, she moved into the aisle and joined people who were beginning to exit.

Max quickly followed her, frustrated with the

direction their exchange had taken. Why couldn't she accept that he cared and was concerned?

# CHAPTER 29

"Dillon!" bellowed Casey, as he saw him coming through the door. "Come in, come in. Where is your sidekick?"

Dillon approached Casey's desk somewhat tentatively. "Uh, Max is in the field, so he couldn't come today."

"The field? Does that mean he is bringing Claire in? Speak up, Man! I want results, and I don't see much happening."

"Well, you see—he and I aren't working together —on this, I mean."

"Now you have me confused. I hired the two of you as my best chance of finding Claire. And now you aren't even looking for her? That won't do, Dillon. That just won't do."

"I understand, Casey. And I think I can assure

you that this is my first priority. I take full responsibility."

"Words, Dillon, words. I want results—and I want them now. I don't want to see you until I see those results. Understood?"

"Understood, sir."

"OK. Get out."

Dillon hurried out as Casey yelled for Maggie to come in.

"Maggie! Oh, come in, Maggie. Close the door. Can you find that P.I., Max? I'm not getting anywhere with the lawyer. I am really worried about Claire, and—"

"Casey!" she interrupted. "I just heard from Max. He and Claire are both coming in to talk with you!"

"Well, where are they? When are the coming? Get them in here pronto!"

"They aren't in the country yet, and—"

"What do you mean? They are out of the country? Where?"

"Casey, I don't know. But he assured me they will be here as soon as they land."

"Huh! Well, I guess that will have to do. What in

the world got into that girl," he puzzled to himself.

"Maybe getting shot at?" Maggie retorted.

"She should have come to me!"

Maggie just looked at him with a slight smile. "Anything else, Casey?"

"No, no. Just get them in here as soon as they arrive."

# CHAPTER 30

Maggie was at her desk as Claire came out of the elevator. She stood as Claire came toward the office. "Claire—Oh, Claire!" she exclaimed, opening her arms to enfold her.

Claire hesitated only a moment. She felt such comfort in Maggie's warm hug.

"We were so scared that something bad had happened to you. Why didn't you call?"

"A lot has happened, including losing my phone," Claire replied as she disengaged herself from Maggie's arms. "Maggie," she hesitated, not sure where she stood. Her emotions were too close to the surface, and she couldn't afford them right now. "Is Casey in there?" She indicated his office.

"Yes, of course. I was about to get his coffee. He wants to see you—be sure you are all right."

Maggie began moving to the office door.

Claire held her back, taking her arm. "Wait—just a minute," she trembled slightly. Why was she so nervous—not nervous! She thought to herself— scared! "OK, thanks, Maggie. I'll always be grateful to you."

Maggie looked at her in astonishment. "Claire—I care for you! Besides, you are my best friend's daughter, a part of Ruthie," she said, almost weeping.

Claire gulped, hoping that Casey felt the same way.

Claire opened the office door and looked at Casey, who was at his desk as she entered. Mustering her resolve, she strode across the room and stood before him.

Casey sat, looking at her. When she was facing him, he stood and limped around the desk. He put his hands on her shoulders before he asked, "You are OK?" She nodded. "Come. Sit," he directed.

Neither said anything as he moved a chair closer to her and sat. Claire didn't know what to do. Her heart was beating so fast she felt dizzy.

"Why did you run, Claire?" he asked in as

neutral a tone as he could muster.

She blurted, "Why should I trust you?"

Casey heard her anxiety, aware of her need for an explanation. "You're my niece."

She stood abruptly as her mouth flew open, no sound emerging.

He said it for her. "Why didn't I tell you?"

"Yes! Tell me at least *that!* You told me *nothing!* You didn't even *talk* to me!" Thoughts swirled in her head. *Her uncle?* She stood facing him, "Where were you when Nana was alive? From the moment you hired me—you lied to me!"

This was not how anyone ever talked to Casey Malone! He was dumbfounded.

Claire paced as she ranted: "Somebody shot at me, tried to kill me! Everybody suspected it was you! And after Henry was pulled out of the Hudson, I thought..." She threw her hands up in the air. She sputtered, "How could you do that? How could—"

He interrupted, roaring, "Who *said* that? I would never try to kill you!" His bum leg kept him from standing quickly. But his eyes burned into hers. They were at a momentary impasse. His voice stopped her in mid-sentence. He continued:

"Let me tell you, Missy, that I have taken care of you since you were born!" he thundered. "When Ruthie was killed—" He choked up for a moment, then continued, "I had one duty: make sure you were safe!"

"Safe from whom?"

"From Sam, who shot your mother!" he spit out.

Claire felt numb. Too much; overloaded, she thought. She fell back onto her chair. "Why didn't you...?"

She shook, trying to regain a semblance of control. "Why didn't you tell me all of this years ago?" she plaintively questioned.

"Your safety! What else?"

"You didn't think I might have needed family? To belong somewhere? With someone? You left me!"

"I did no such thing!" He quieted. "I made sure you and Nana had everything you needed."

"Except your presence, your affection?" she said sarcastically.

Casey huffed. "Tell me; How were you able to go to good schools? Where did your good clothes come from? Did you ever go hungry?" He waited, pinning her in her chair with his eyes.

Claire squirmed, trying to avoid looking at him directly. "Couldn't you have at least told me about my mother? You say you were close—"

"I adored your mother!" he yelled. "I took care of her, protected her—until that bastard, Sam, took her away from me." He cringed at that memory, his breath coming heavy and deep.

She looked at him with different eyes. He could not have tried to kill her. She knew that now. But... "If only you had told me, or even let Maggie tell me, all this confusion—"

"I couldn't and still protect you. Family, the neighborhood—that's my mission. I will do anything to protect that. I couldn't let Sam know you are my niece. Ruthie hid you from him. I had to do the same."

The quiet felt almost startling. Claire looked at him, needing to know, but unsure how to ask, "But the man who was found in the river, it was Henry! I thought—" she gulped, ready to ask more, but she was interrupted by Casey.

"Sam! Huh! He's hell-bent on taking out my people!" Casey looked at Claire. "He will be taken care of. Nothing for you to worry about."

Claire knew she would have to be content with

that answer. "So," she almost whispered, "What do I call you? Uncle? Casey? Mr. Malone?"

"Oh, for goodness' sake, Claire," irritated at her question. "How about *boss!* At least, while you work here," he grumped.

"I still work here?" She was incredulous.

"Safest place; keep my eyes on you," he said gruffly.

They sat side by side, each processing this stage of events.

It dawned on her that he knew nothing about the deposition.

"So, what do we do now?" she asked.

"You work—here. And if you have questions, you ask! Don't go around making up stories about me or what I do! I won't have it!" he blustered.

"Who should I ask? You? Maggie?"

Casey muttered to himself before he said to her, "Me—Maggie—doesn't matter, just remember: loyalty is everything, whether I'm your boss or uncle or friend. Just don't forget that."

Claire felt guilt along with relief, knowing the deposition was never made.

He glared at her, then waved her to the door. The confrontation was over—at least, for now.

Before she left, she walked over to him, holding out her hand, "Thanks—Boss. Uncle."

He took her hand, and when he looked up, he saw that she was trying to smile.

Claire left with a firm stride, closing the door gently but firmly behind her.

# CHAPTER 31

As the door shut behind her, Claire leaned against it, her eyes shining, smiling at Maggie. Suddenly the elevator doors opened, revealing Max hurrying toward her. She reached her arms out to him, almost crying. Relieved and happy, she said to them both: "I did it! I really did it. I talked to him, and it's OK!" Her hands flew to her mouth as she exclaimed, "I can't believe it! Max, oh, Max —You were right. My *uncle* didn't try to kill me!" She was almost giddy, hearing how ridiculous that sounded to her own ears.

Max laughed with her, then sobered when he understood what she was saying. Her uncle? The realization hit him: She *doesn't need me* to rescue her.

*God!* He sounded like he was talking about

Dillon.

He moved away as Claire rushed to hug Maggie.

"It's not finished yet, but it's going to be OK!" Claire exclaimed to her.

Maggie just gazed at the ecstatic face in front of her. At last, she asked, "You really are OK? You're sure you aren't hurt."

Calming, Claire smiled at her, nodded yes, and then turned to face Max, only to discover he was gone. "Where did he go?" she asked.

"I don't know, Honey. I think he just left."

"Why? Why would he do that? Now? I need—" She paused, rethinking what she was about to say. Did she need him, or just want him? She believed she could really trust him now. Why did he leave? Had she misinterpreted his attentions?

She turned to Maggie, "I apologize for worrying you, for not saying anything. I just ran without thinking about anyone else."

Maggie gave her another hug. "It's all right, Honey. Are you going to stay?"

"Oh, yes. Casey actually welcomed me back! Well, maybe not *welcomed*," she said with a little laugh. Pulling herself together, she told Maggie, "I need to go home to take care of some things. Then,

I'll be back bright and early tomorrow morning."

"Take as much time as you need," Maggie said, grinning happily. "We'll get together and plan out your work schedule."

* * *

Max left, confused, and a little lost. He had given Dillon such a hard time about falling for the damsel-in-distress syndrome. And here he was doing the same damn thing.

Is that all Claire was to him? A beautiful distraction? Maybe he really was just tying up loose ends. He left the elevator and headed outside. He was trying to decide where he was going when he left the two women hugging each other. Why did that bother him so much?

Max caught a taxi and directed the driver to Dillon's old office. He needed to clear the air between them, and also let him know all that had happened—well most of it, anyway. He should at least do that.

* * *

Once Claire had left, Maggie tapped on Casey's door. "Come in, come in," he barked.

As Maggie entered Casey's office, she saw her boss rubbing his head with both hands, obviously disturbed. What had happened between them?

Casey looked up. "Maggie, what is with that girl? I do everything I can to protect her, take care of her, and she's mad at me! No gratitude—at all!"

"I think she was just shocked that you, *her uncle*, always has been protecting her," Maggie's responded, trying to smooth her boss's ruffled feathers.

"Huh." Leaning back in his high-backed chair, he asked, "How could I tell her, Maggie? Look how Sam has reacted? His own daughter!" he yelled, fist pounding on the desk.

"But Sam doesn't know that though, does he?" she asked. "What was his intention, anyway?"

"To hurt me, of course. If he found out—" The realization hit him. "Maggie, Claire could still be in danger." He practically sputtered, "Maggie, get that kid—you know—"

"Bobby?"

"Yeah, get him in here. I need to find out what Sam really knows—or doesn't know. And then I've got to decide what I'm going to do about this little shite, Bobby."

"I'm on it," she said as she left.

# CHAPTER 32

Casey slumped, exhausted in his chair. His eyes closed. So many memories flooded back, painful, confusing memories. He would never forget coming home late that night, climbing the narrow stairs, stopping when he heard an awful retching sound coming from the bathroom. He raced up the rest of the stairs, threw open the bathroom door, and found Ruthie puking her guts out.

"Oh, Ruthie!" He had gently pulled her hair away from her face and rubbed her back until she was finished.

She sat back on the floor, moaning as she realized it was her brother. "I didn't want you to see this!" she sobbed. "I don't know what to do."

"You're sick, you'll get better," he tried to reassure her. "Don't worry, just—"

"Casey! Stop! I'm pregnant! It's not going to get *better!*"

"Pregnant? Who? Who did this to you?"

"Oh, Casey," she plaintively cried, "Who do you think?"

"Not Sam! I told him to never come near you. *You* said you never wanted to see him again!"

"A lot of good that did!"

Casey looked at her, then sat down beside her on the floor. "Ruthie—when?"

"Maybe two, three months ago. I haven't seen him since. Casey, he terrified me. He was so angry... I had no choice." Her sobbing began again. "I am so sorry!"

"Ruthie, this is not your fault. Stop crying, please. We'll figure something out."

He took a wet cloth and tenderly wiped her face then asked, "Does Sam know?"

"NO! And you can't tell him! You just can't!"

"No, no. Of course not. Come on, you should lie down," Casey said as he helped her up off the floor. "I'll rustle up some grub. OK? Gotta keep your strength up!"

Once Ruthie was in bed and curled up with her comforter, Casey went downstairs to the kitchen.

He found a can of soup in the pantry that he could heat up for her.

What in the heck could he do? Ruthie and Nana were not safe here. Sam would find out for sure. *That Could Not Happen!*

He took the soup up to her, pasting a smile on his face as he entered her room.

Opening his eyes, dispelling his vivid memory, Casey straightened up in his desk chair, resolved. This time Sam would pay.

# CHAPTER 33

Maggie burst into Casey's office without knocking. He was standing, looking out of the floor-to-ceiling window, seeing nothing, slightly bent over, leaning on his cane.

She cleared her throat, "Casey?"

He turned slowly, finally acknowledging her. "What's wrong, Maggie?"

"It's Bobby," she said anxiously. "He's gone; nobody knows where he is; nobody's seen him. I sent our people to check the room he rents. The lock was broken! His stuff was still there, but his clothes were gone." She stopped, waiting for him to say something.

"Maggie, sit down." He moved to the couch and sat facing her. He paused for a few moments, making her wonder what was coming. "Bobby is probably dead," he said. "You and I know we had nothing to do with that," he said sharply, looking directly at her as he waited for her acknowledgment.

She nodded, then dropped her head until she said, "But who? Why?"

"Bobby was working for Sam. Our little friend, Bobby, was a mole."

Maggie gasped, "Oh, no! So, Bobby's been lying to us this whole time?"

"I've confirmed all that Claire told me. Turns out, Sam was out to get me through Claire." His voice turned bitter.

Maggie sat stunned, feeling Casey's anguish.

"Claire must be protected, Maggie. She is angry at me—for keeping her safe!" Casey exhaled loudly. "And that makes it all the harder to do," he grumped. "She thinks I 'abandoned' her." He stiffly turned toward Maggie, and with his cane, walked to his desk chair. Before he sat, he leaned on the desk and said, forcefully, "I *had* to keep her away from me! It was the only way to keep her and Nana safe!"

Casey sat and slumped in the chair. He shook his head but said nothing more.

"Couldn't you tell her that," asked Maggie.

"I did. She's not listening—to me, anyway." He looked up at her. "Maggie?"

"Yes, of course. I'll make her understand. But, should I tell her about Bobby? And what about Sam?"

"Not that he is her father," he said firmly. "About Bobby—whatever you think best."

"OK." Maggie turned to go. "But Casey—"

He sighed, "I'll tell her myself when the time is right."

"All right. I'll let you know how it goes."

# CHAPTER 34

*MONTHS LATER...*

Claire was back at work, but her heart wasn't really in it. Almost everything she was assigned was in-house. She knew Casey was concerned with her safety, but she felt confined.

Casey had asked Maggie to find her a different apartment—in essence, a 'safe house.' Annoying, but she was in no position to complain. She still met with clients, but always in-house—no more dinner assignments. Maggie filled that position, although it wasn't too often.

She thought she had put Max out of her mind. That had been hard. Max and Dillon had gone out of their way to protect her. Her own self-absorption had blinded her.

And Max! He just disappeared from her life. She finally had begun to let her feelings show and

Boom! Gone. She showed him she was no longer running. And then he runs off!

She could hardly blame him. Their behavior didn't exactly predict a great relationship. But that was exactly what she wanted: a chance to have a real relationship—with him! Swallowing her pride, she had actually phoned him several times; and always the same voice mail message: *Not available.*

At the computer, Claire fished up the final report on the last couple she'd interviewed and printed it out to give Maggie. She popped her laptop into her briefcase and left work for home—such as it was. She really missed that first apartment—but no complaints! She reminded herself.

Maggie thanked Claire as she took the report from her. "Have a good night," she called after her.

"Thanks, I will. You too."

# CHAPTER 35

Dillon decided on lunch by himself, but not in the office. Too many interruptions. Casey had kept him pretty busy over these last few months, and he wanted to chill out. He had found a little deli just around the corner that not too many colleagues knew about. He had ordered and settled himself when the restaurant door swung open.

As he looked up, he was surprised to see Claire enter. She was alone and apparently not familiar with the place.

Looking for an available table, her eyes found him. She hesitated, apparently deciding whether to leave or stay.

Dillon beckoned her over. "How are you?" he asked as he stood, waiting for her to sit down.

"Small world—" she began.

He smiled. "This is my special hideout."

She smiled back—more politely than friendly. "Is the food any good?" she asked.

"It's more the quiet and seclusion that recommends it than the food," he admitted. "How are you, Claire? We haven't run into each other even though we work in the same building." The waitress arrived with his lunch.

Glad for the interruption, she motioned that he should go ahead; not wait for her. She quickly ordered a small salad and an ice tea. "I hadn't expected to find anyone I know here," she said.

"I guess we were both looking for the same thing," he quipped.

"Dillon—" "Claire—" They each said at the same time.

They both smiled, somewhat embarrassed.

"OK, you first," he said.

"I hear you are still working for Casey," Claire said. "How is it working for him?"

Dillon had taken a bite of his sandwich, shrugged, swallowed, and replied, "Better than I might have expected."

"Oh? I am glad to hear that," she said as her salad and drink arrived. After a few bites, she asked, "Have you seen Max lately?"

"We haven't talked in a while."

Seeing her surprised expression, he asserted, "It's fine. He passed the bar and then decided to take a sabbatical." Dillon laughed, somewhat uncomfortably.

"Oh, that's wonderful," Claire said without much enthusiasm. "I know that really matters to him."

"I take it that you and he aren't...?" Dillon asked.

"No, no. We just, sort of, parted ways." She focused on the salad in front of her.

"Claire, I'm sorry things got so messed up, and —"

"No, really, there's no problem. I'm happy you are doing well, and Max—I hope he is as well." Claire paused and then said, "If you should see him... you know, run into him, please let him know —" She stopped, and cleared her throat. "Let him know I wish him well." She pulled back her chair, stood—placing some dollars on the table. "I really need to get back. Dillon, thanks for everything. I don't think I ever had a chance to say that." She smiled briefly at him and left quickly.

*Whoa*, thought Dillon as he watched her hurry out. She is really hurting—over Max! That was a surprise. Max never said anything about a relationship. Is that why he took off? Well, he hoped he would find out that Claire still cared. He beckoned the waitress, paid, and left the rest of his lunch uneaten.

# CHAPTER 36

Max couldn't find any peace, even after passing the dreaded bar exam. Right after the results were posted, he had fled to his sanctuary, thinking he could now just kick back, relax as he decided his next steps. He had managed to keep thoughts about Claire tucked away while preparing for the bar exam. That was no longer working.

He knew he needed to reflect, think things through. But he was so agitated he couldn't sit still. His constant pacing wasn't helping. He couldn't sleep. Booze was useless.

His thoughts just kept revolving in ongoing loops, always about Claire. Why had Claire just barged ahead—without him? No, that wasn't the issue he admitted to himself. He felt useless, which was stupid, but it was how he felt. Pride? Yeah, more likely. He didn't like knowing that. Unproductively, his thoughts just kept spinning in circles.

Exhaustion finally took over, and he slept. Disturbing dreams finally woke him. And after a strong cup of coffee, he began thinking again about Claire.

*"Admit it! You care for her!"*

Her anger, her impulsiveness couldn't override the vulnerability he saw in her—that made him want to take her in his arms, make her feel safe. He poured himself another cup of coffee. And, yes, he admired her! Her courage. She charged ahead, right into Casey's office, not knowing how he would react to her demand for the whole story. Damn, he hadn't anticipated that. He was so proud of her spirit. So, why did he feel so left out?

It was clear Casey wasn't the problem anymore. He sat with that for a while, sipping his now lukewarm coffee.

Suddenly, he sat straight up, put the cup down. He had got so enmeshed in his own emotions, he had lost sight of the real danger—Sam! He was still out there. He might try to hurt Claire again.

Max's last fruitless call to Claire resulted in his

hearing: "This is a disconnected number." Calls to her office phone were deflected by her assistant. Frustrated, he decided to go after her in person.

Max hurried back to the City. But when he tried to enter Casey's building, he was stopped at the entrance.

"But I have to see Ms. Cousins," he exploded at the guard.

"I'll check that for you, sir, but no one goes up who isn't authorized." The guard was adamant. "And you aren't on the list."

Max twitched with anxiety, but in taking a look at the skeptical guard, he forced himself to calm down.

The guard had disconnected his Bluetooth and was turning away. "Ms. Cousins is not available, sir."

"Casey," Max said. "Let me speak with Casey Malone."

"That's who I *did* speak with, sir, No dice! Now, please move along."

Max gulped. Losing his cool was not going to help. "May I leave a message—for either of them?"

The guard studied him. "I guess that will be OK."

"Great! I'll be back shortly," said Max as he retreated. He headed for the nearby cafe. *What can I say?* He thought. *Who should I write?*

He ordered coffee and sat, pen, and pad in hand.

Once he had dropped off the note for Casey as well as one for Claire, he decided to try Claire's apartment. He thought the doorman would be willing to take a note to her. However, it was the doorman who told him she no longer lived there.

Casey must be trying to keep her under wraps, he realized. So, he was concerned about her safety too! Finally, the rejection of his attempted visit began to make sense. Security had increased considerably.

*I wonder what Dillon knows*, he thought. "*If* he will speak to me..."

Max remembered that while Dillon had taken an office in Casey's building, he still had kept his old place for independent work. He would try him there first.

Max trundled up the stairs to Dillon's office. Hoping that Dillon could provide a lead to finding Claire, he rapped on the door, then entered. "Hi

Dillon."

"Max! Hey, come on in." He gave Max a man-hug.

"Way too long! Grab a cup of coffee. I finally splurged for a great coffee maker," he said, all in a rush and semblance of a laugh.

Max looked around, noting the new carpet on the floor, the new desk, and chairs—even an original abstract on the wall. "Looks like things have looked up."

"Yeah, right? About time, huh?"

"I'm glad for you, Dillon," he said, but what he was thinking was, *It all feels wrong—the office, the superficial "welcome."*

Dillon sat down behind his over-sized desk: "Sit down, Max! Please, sit down."

Max decided to ignore his discomfort and get to the point. It was clear that things would never be the same between them. "I just came by to see if you could help me reach Claire. I need to talk to her, but she seems to have moved. Can you get me her new address, or into the office building?" Max felt more and more awkward.

"Yeah, about that... Look, I'll level with you, Max. Casey made conditions for working for him:

no more partnership; no contact with Claire—for either of us. I know it's kind of weird, but he has her securely locked up—not literally, but definitely incommunicado. Sit Max, please. You are making me uncomfortable."

Dejected, Max sat. "How am I ever going to talk her?"

At Max's bereft expression, Dillon offered, "I accidentally ran into Claire at a restaurant recently. I hadn't seen her in months. She seemed fine... asked me to tell you, if I ran into you, that she wishes you the best." Dillon could see that this wasn't what Max wanted to hear.

"Let me talk to Casey," Dillon urged, "Maybe he will relent. Anyway, let me try. OK?"

# CHAPTER 37

Max was determined to get clear with Claire. He couldn't wait for Dillon's proffered help. He had to see Casey and convince him to let him talk to Claire. He would try one more time. In spite of his misgivings, he once again made his way to Casey's office building.

This time luck was on his side. The guard had sneaked out for a quick smoke, so Max grabbed the opportunity to catch the opening door of the elevator. Exiting, he greeted Maggie, who was ready to block him from approaching Casey's office.

"I have to see him! Claire is in danger!"

Alarmed, Maggie opened Casey's door to let him enter, then quickly shut it behind him.

Max stood until Casey beckoned him in.

"What is this all about?" Casey snarled.

"You have to protect Claire!" Max urged.

"What do you think I've been doing?"

"I know, I know. But *I'm* not the one who wants to hurt her. Sam is!"

"What do you know about Sam?" Casey bellowed back.

"Not enough!"

Casey stared at Max, trying to size him up. *Maybe this is the guy I should be talking to.* "Talk to me."

"I need to know about Sam. I have to see Claire. Talk to her."

Casey nodded.

Max stared at him, making sure the nod was a yes before continuing. "Claire said Bobby told her *Sam hired the hit*. But I need evidence. It's the only way I can prosecute."

"Evidence? Huh. History—you don't know him without knowing his history." He pointed Max to a chair, not saying anything more.

A far-off look came over Casey's face.

"Please. Tell me about Sam."

"He and I were best buds. You know, as young

kids. He was the risk-taker. If you dare him to do anything, off he goes. But, what a temper. Fights got him into trouble all the time. Probably because he was an Italian kid living in an Irish neighborhood.

"Anyway, by the time we hit high school, he grew up. I mean literally. Six foot, black wavy hair. Boy, was he proud of that hair. Icy blue eyes," Casey chuckled. "The girls were all over him." He sat, staring into old memories. "Suddenly, he had bucks in his pocket. Later, I found out he was gambling—a lot. And winning, I guess.

"He wanted to rope me into his schemes, but no way was I going that route. And we started to drift apart, except—Ruthie, my kid sister—they were starting to hang out together before I knew anything about it. I didn't like it, but Ruthie was smitten and didn't want to hear about all the other dolls who were at his beck and call.

"When I found out, she begged me to go on a double date with them. I said OK, reluctantly; I even asked Maggie along. Everything seemed OK until some SOB's started giving us trouble. I had never seen him so riled up. He had a gun! Out with my sister, and he had a gun on him! I pulled him back as those idiots took off. Ruthie was really shaken up. I hoped that she might be scared enough to stay away from him. But they were a lot closer than I knew, and Sam was persistent." He stopped, seemingly lost in his memories. "I threatened him; told him to stay away."

Max cleared his throat, wondering if he should interrupt his musings.

But Casey straightened up, took a deep breath, and continued, "He's in the gambling business full-time these days. Always on the move—that guy never could stay still. He's got connections, agreements with syndicates all over the States. He's off to the West Coast—you know, Vegas, Reno, even L.A. where he's hooked up with one of the cartels. On the East Coast—Atlantic City, of course. New York is his home base.

"We've managed to stay out of each other's way —at least, until recently. He told me himself that he put the hit on Claire. He *thought* he killed her. He shot *me* as a warning. I'm pretty sure he killed Henry, my employee. Any operation that tries to move into his territory can expect to be eliminated. No one is allowed on his turf."

Casey took a hard look at Max. "He does not

know that Claire is his daughter; I made sure of that." Max leaned forward, wanting to quiz him, but Casey interrupted: "We moved Ruthie and Mom away before he had any idea Ruthie was pregnant. I really thought we were finished—he and I."

Max asked, "Does Claire know that...?"

"No! And you are not to tell her! I don't know what she would do if she found out that he was her father. I don't know that I could protect her if he found out. What if she decided to go after Sam? What would he do? I'm sure he caused Ruthie's death. He *already* tried to have Claire killed just to get to me!"

"You know that? For sure?"

"He confessed!"

"What about this Bobby she was dating for a while? Sounds like he was the trigger man. If we could get him to confess..."

"No. He's gone. Out of the picture." Casey pointed his finger at Max as he said, "Not by me just so you know! And now you know about Sam. You have some plan I don't know about?"

"My only plan is to make sure Claire is safe, whatever it takes."

"That's it?" Casey huffed.

"I also want her, and you, to know that I love her, and I will do everything in my power to not only keep her safe but to make her happy."

"Huh. I see. Does she have any idea?"

"Not... not all of it. Look! I'm not about to ask you for your blessing—"

"OK. OK. Don't get huffy," Casey grumbled. "Maybe, we should join forces to protect Claire."

"If we can work together," Max nodded, "that would be... acceptable."

"Huh! OK. Get out of here and come back with a plan. If I get a fantastic idea, I'll let you know!" Casey said, somewhat sarcastically.

Max was happy to oblige.

\* \* \*

As soon as Dillon got the word that Max was no longer persona non grata, he called Max. Not getting an answer, he left a voice message. "I need to see you. Don't worry, it's *good* news!"

Dillon was relieved and happy when Max came through his door. He smiled and waved him to a seat. Wasting no time, he began, "When we talked... Do you remember that I told you I accidentally ran into Claire at this little out-of-the-way deli, where we started to have lunch together until she just ran off?"

Surprised, Max asked, "Sure. Of course, I remember. Why?"

"Well, when we started talking about you, she got very teary." He paused, watching Max's response. "I wanted to tell you then, Max. She's hurting—She really cares for you and doesn't understand what happened between you. Heck! I don't understand! What did happen?" he asked.

Max gathered his confused thoughts before answering. "The short version is that when we got back from Costa Rica, she just bolted, and on her own, she had a showdown with Casey!"

"So?" Dillon was puzzled.

"It was very clear she no longer needed my help —or me." The last had been hard to admit. "I was proud of her," he emphasized. "I realized I had to get out of her way, so I left," he said somewhat sheepishly.

"Max, I think you got it wrong. She asked me where you were and anything I could tell her about you. It wasn't much."

"My bad. I'm sorry about that."

"Not a problem," Dillon reassured. "I know you needed your space."

"I'm afraid for her, Dillon," Max said. "I know that Casey won't hurt her. He cares for her. That's why he keeps her under wraps. It is *Sam* we have to be afraid of!"

"I heard that you were able to see Casey."

"That's how I know about Sam."

"OK. Let me see what I can do to help. No one is safe until we figure out how to stop Sam."

Max looked skeptical, but Dillon persisted: "Come on, Max—let me help. How many times have you bailed me out of awful situations? Huh?"

"Thanks." Max took Dillon's outstretched hand.

# CHAPTER 38

Maggie and Claire were in the alcove, getting coffee, taking a break. Claire, hoping this might be an opportune time to question Maggie, asked, "Maggie, why won't you or Casey talk to me about my mother? I was so little when she died—when she was killed."

"Too painful for Casey. For me, too, I guess." She placed her hand on her heart. "We were like sisters, we were so close."

Claire could see her remembering. "Please, I know so little." She reached for Maggie's hand. "Just tell me more about what she was like?"

Maggie looked at Claire's stricken face. She took a sip of her coffee before she said, "Casey always saw himself as her protector. So, when she was killed—" Maggie stopped, then put her arm around

Claire. "She was so pretty—very petite. Her hair was a little lighter than yours, but she had the same pixie nose. She seemed fragile, but she was a lot stronger than Casey could ever see. I see a lot of her in you—her strength, especially when—" She paused again. "She adored you. You were everything she ever wanted." Maggie choked up, "I missed her so much when she, Casey, and their mom moved away."

Claire started to ask about her father, but they were interrupted by Casey's bark: "Maggie!"

"Why can't he just buzz the intercom?" Maggie sighed and hurried into his office.

"Damn." Claire returned to her own office, muttering to herself, frustrated.


As Maggie hurried into his office, she blurted, "Casey—Boss!" He looked up from the papers he had been reading.

"Maggie, I need you to take these to the—" He took in her expression. "What's the matter?"

"Casey—we have to tell Claire about Sam!"

# CHAPTER 39

Claire couldn't sit still. The reports could wait. She headed for the elevator.

Maggie would get them before the deadline. She pushed the button for the cafeteria in the basement level. The elevator whisked her down without a stop.

She hurriedly stepped out of the elevator and almost ran into a man trying to get in. She looked up and then quickly moved back through the still-open door.

"Max!" Claire almost choked; she was so astounded.

Max was holding the door open, "Claire, please, talk to me. I've tried so hard to reach you?"

"You have?" She moved further back, giving him room to enter. The doors closed behind him.

"Didn't you receive my messages?" he asked. They hadn't pressed any button yet.

"You sent me a message?" She coughed nervously, "Where to?"

Max pressed the lobby button. "Let's just get out of here," he urged.

She knew Casey wouldn't like her leaving the building unescorted—of course, she *would* be escorted, she smiled to herself. Just not by the usual bodyguard, and he wouldn't come to get her until she rang him. "All right. Let's go."

It wasn't crowded on the street; too early for the lunch rush, but Max hurried Claire along. It was hard to keep up with him and his long legs. "Where..." she began as he veered them to the right into a tiny tea shop. The smells of cinnamon and other spices filled the small space.

He headed for a small table in the back and pulled a chair out for her. She sat, wondering what was happening.

Before he joined her, he turned to the tiny lady behind a glass counter that displayed many kinds of tea as well as a variety of unusual pastries. He ordered a pot of her special tea. She smiled and immediately began preparing the somewhat exotic smelling tea.

Max smiled at Claire as he sat down. "I hope you are OK with this."

"It feels a little cloak and dagger," she tried to joke.

He acknowledged her description, "Yes, doesn't it?" The pot of tea was placed on the table. "I hope you like this," he said as the tiny proprietor poured the tea into delicate porcelain cups. He thanked her and turned again to Claire.

"Why wouldn't Casey let you see me or even contact me?" he asked.

Claire put her hands around her fragile cup and breathed in the spicy aroma before answering. "He wanted to know where I had gone, what had happened. I didn't know what to tell him." She glanced at Max before saying, "Maybe he got the idea that you had hurt me in some way." She hesitated, but then continued, "I thought—when you left, I thought... I mean... I don't know what I thought," she finally stated.

"I just assumed—"

"Always a mistake," she retorted.

"I thought you and Casey worked it out; you

didn't need me—my help anymore. Assignment finished."

"Is that all I was, an assignment?" she blurted. She glanced away from him, not happy she had let that slip. She took a sip of her tea, trying to recover her composure, not looking at him.

Max saw the tears running down Claire's cheek. He took her hand. She was beyond saying anything. He stood and pulled her to her feet and enclosed her in his arms. He held her close as she buried her face in his chest. She nodded at his proffered handkerchief.

Their silence grew until the tiny lady came over to see if they wanted anything else. She had startled them both. Gently, she placed a hand on Claire's shoulder, and then her other hand on Max's shoulder. She smiled at each of them and left, disappearing behind a curtained doorway.

Max released Claire to pay for the tea, but the tiny lady poked her head out of the curtained doorway to signal that they owed nothing. With a smile and a little wave goodbye, she disappeared once again behind the curtain.

# CHAPTER 40

They walked for a time, lost in their own thoughts. As they approached a small park, nestled next to one of the City's old churches, Max took her hand and pulled her with him toward a secluded bench.

She acquiesced, appreciating the calm this place seemed to induce.

"You've seen some of my favorite secret spots today," he said to her, smiling.

"You have more?" she asked, smiling back at him.

"Hm—maybe a few," he replied.

"Like your beautiful home," she said, remembering how she had run from that place.

He didn't comment.

"Max, I'm so sorry—"

"Let's not go there," he said, patting her hand. "This is where we are now. Yes?"

She looked up at him beside her on the bench. Tentatively she asked, "Where exactly is that?"

Max sighed, knowing he had to shift the conversation, perhaps ruining this lovely moment together.

Once again, he took her hand. "Claire," he began, "I'm very concerned about you and your safety."

She withdrew her hand. "Did Casey send you?" her voice reflecting hurt and suspicion. "Are you just on a job?"

"Of course not! He wouldn't even let me see you. Or contact you!"

She eased back a little, realizing that what he said was true.

"Look, Claire. You were almost killed! And Casey was not the bad guy, yes?"

She nodded.

"We think Sam is still a threat."

Claire interrupted, "We?"

"I've talked with Casey. And before you get upset —"

Claire stood and took a step before he took her arm. "And I think both of us—yes, *you and I*," Max emphasized, "should talk to him together."

She stopped and turned back to him. "Why?"

"There are things you need to know, and it's not up to me to disclose."

"That sounds cryptic!"

"Please, Claire. Trust me—one more time," Max pleaded.

Claire felt his sincerity and sat again. "All right. We'll talk to Casey, but I thought he wouldn't see you?" Her curiosity aroused. "What changed?"

"I insisted. Come on. Let's face the old lion in his den," he quipped.

"Lion?"

"Just an expression."

# CHAPTER 41

Maggie warned Casey that he had two visitors and then stepped aside to let Max and Claire into Casey's office.

Max announced as they came in, "We need to talk with you, Casey. The two of us."

"So... Come in. Sit. The couch," he directed. "What is so urgent you just burst in—"

"We didn't burst!" Claire loudly insisted.

Casey waved them to sit on the couch. He watched and drew his own conclusions about their relationship. "So, you come to ask my blessing?" he snorted. "Huh?"

"NO!" came from each of them simultaneously.

Max spoke first, "She needs to know—for her safety and peace of mind—what we discussed. It should come from you."

Claire inserted herself into the conversation, "Why have you kept me walled off from everyone—from Max!"

"Your safety! Of course," Casey barked. He limped back to his big chair.

"I thought the threat was over!" Her emotions escaping her control.

"Sam doesn't let anything go!" Casey roared, increasingly agitated with her. "Who do you think shot me?"

"Who in the hell is this *SAM?* And why would he care about *me* at all?" She was fed up with the secrets, the ambiguity, all of it.

Max looked pointedly at Casey, waiting.

Casey stared at both of them, and then said, "Sam is your father."

Stunned, she found it hard to breathe, let alone speak. "My *father* wants to kill me?!"

"No! He doesn't know!" Max butted in.

"But, *you* know?" Her eyes widened. "Well, I guess it's time Sam knows too since everybody knows except him and me!"

She started to rise until Casey broke in, "Sit down, Claire! That is not the whole story."

"What else is there, Casey? You've kept the most

important person in my life a secret from me! And I can clear up this mess right now. All I have to do is tell him! Don't you see? I won't be a target anymore."

Max tried to restrain her outburst, "Claire, please, just listen for once!"

"Whose side are you on?" she exclaimed. Her flushed face showed her hurt and confusion.

"This is not a love story, Claire!" Casey bellowed. "We are talking about my abused sister, who was *raped*! To protect you, we moved you away. Sam never knew. And he *never will!*"

"My mother was—?" Claire couldn't bring herself to say it.

"Raped. You heard me correctly."

All three sat, silenced.

Claire broke the silence, asking in a quavering voice, "Why haven't you told me this before? Why wouldn't you tell me that when I first came to work for you—Who ARE you?" her voice breaking, the tears beginning. "I want to meet my father! I want to hear *his* side. Neither of you seems able to tell me the truth!"

Casey and Max anxiously tried to placate her. She was having none of it. She got up and practically sprinted across the room.

They shouted, moving after her. Max reached her first, pleading, "Please, just listen, Claire."

She hesitated, staring at both of them. She then walked deliberately back and sat once more.

Casey gave in. "It was important that you had no connection to me. He could have taken you—especially after Ruthie died. He blamed me for keeping Ruthie from him." Her expression told him that wouldn't satisfy her.

"OK, here it is." Casey launched into his story:

"We were all friends as kids. He got mixed up with bad people, and I wanted no part of them. Ruthie seemed to have a calming effect over him—at first—that is until we were almost run over by his so-called friends. He went after them, ready to attack them... he was acting so crazy he terrified Ruthie. She ran. When I found her at home, shaking, she begged me to keep Sam from her. Turns out, she had tried to break it off before, but he got so angry she gave up. I promised that he would never get close to her again."

"But, then how—?" she probed.

"Yeah. I didn't know until it was too late. He

could lay on the charm. Ruthie tried to resist—and then she couldn't; he wasn't about to take no for an answer. We moved away as soon as we knew you were on your way." Casey's face had turned ashen. It was the first time Claire had seen Casey look defeated.

"I am *so* sorry," Claire said. "But maybe he really *loved* her," she said, wanting desperately to erase the image of rape.

"She loved YOU, not HIM! She adored you, would do anything to make you happy—to just hear you giggle."

Max asked, "So, what do we do, Casey?"

"We have to get rid of Sam."

Both Max and Claire gasped.

Casey continued, "But he can't know it is us."

Max, troubled, asked, "Get rid of—"

"Nah, in spite of what you think," Casey said, looking at their expressions, "I don't bump people off. More subtle than that. I'm working on a plan. Don't worry, Claire. You just stay out of sight until I can get it worked out.

Claire stared at Casey, stunned at this dismissal.

Casey urged Max, "Go, Max, go! I'll call you when I'm ready," At Claire's expression, he admonished her, "Just go to work as usual." He turned back to his desk.

Subduing her anger, she stood and said very distinctly to Casey, "I'm going to meet my father." Ignoring Max's attempt to stop her, she finished, "And I don't need permission from either of you!" With that, she turned and left.

Max hurriedly followed her out.

"Just go to work!" she huffed as she entered the elevator.

Max called after her, "Claire—"

"No—I don't want your *input,* Max. You males just get together and let me know when you've figured out *my* life. Oh, don't forget to remind me how to feel!"

As the elevator door closed, she reiterated to herself: *No more running. I don't do that anymore!*

Max gave up trying to catch up with her. She wasn't going to listen to anything he had to say.


As determined as Claire was to get the real story about Sam, she recognized that she didn't know anything about Sam Salvatore. Maggie! She would know. She grew up with Casey and Sam. Maybe she shouldn't have stormed out of the office without thinking this through.

*I know,* she thought, *I'll ask her to dinner.*

# CHAPTER 42

Opening her door to let Maggie in, she embraced her, saying, "I'm so glad you agreed to come."

Maggie smiled, offering the bottle of red wine she'd brought, "How could I say no to a home-cooked meal?"

"Thank you, Maggie. So thoughtful. The wine will make a simple meal festive."

So formal, thought Maggie, as she shrugged out of her coat.

Claire felt awkward, knowing she had an agenda, but she pushed forward. She guided Maggie into the living-dining area. "Please, make yourself comfortable. The pasta is ready, and the salad is on the table. I hope this is OK. Oh, I almost forgot the bread in the warming oven."

Once seated, the wine poured, compliments

made, Maggie looked at Claire with affection. "OK, Claire. What's on your mind?"

Claire looked up from her plate, surprised at Maggie's accurate intuition.

"Honey, I know you by now. What gives?"

Claire pushed her plate away. "Oh, Maggie, this is hard to say. I know you are totally loyal to Casey —"

"But, you are still wondering..." Claire nodded. "You must know he cares about you and would give his life to protect you."

"No, Maggie. I don't know that."

"Claire, Casey has spent his life protecting his family in any and every way he can. Even when Ruthie got pregnant, he made sure she and Nana were safe—and moved them away to keep you safe."

Abruptly, Claire stopped her. "Why didn't she go to the police if she was raped? Why didn't she get an abortion? Do you really believe his story?" She stopped to take a sip of her wine before she continued, "I'd sure like to hear Sam's version."

Shaking her head in exasperation, Maggie cut her off, "You never had to live like the rest of us. And it sounds to me that Casey made a mistake when he made sure you didn't have to!"

"That's not fair!"

"Where is your loyalty? Ruthie would never have let you know how you came on this earth. She adored you. But I sure wonder how she would feel about you turning on the one person she loved above anyone else!"

"Except Sam? My *father*?"

"You want to know about Sam? Well, let me tell you: His father was a drunk and liked nothing better than to punch him at every opportunity. His mother—I wouldn't even call a mother. He had a reason for his hate. But, he could be very, very charming. He could have had any girl in the neighborhood, but Ruthie was the one he wanted; sweet and innocent." Her voice had turned bitter. "But when something or someone went against Sam, he got violent, even cruel. Her rejection made him crazy, and he decided it was all Casey's fault.

"Although Ruthie begged Casey to keep Sam away from her, he tracked her down. He pleaded with her, but when she said NO! He turned on her, and... Well, you were the result."

"Was it Casey or Ruthie who told you this?" asked Claire, still trying to hold on to her skepticism.

"I was with her when she found out she was pregnant! And when she had you! I knew everything. I had to." Frustrated, Maggie rose from the table. "I have to go. I'm afraid I've lost my appetite." She gathered her coat and handbag and left.

Claire sat, looking at the uneaten food. She knew she had made a mess of the evening and perhaps lost a dear friend—a friend of her mother. Still, it was more than hard to accept their version of her inception. She'd lost her mother when she was five, so early. And just as she thought she had found her father, they want to keep her from him.

Her anger bubbled up again. I am not going to *run* this time. *No matter what, I'm going to meet him! I'll see for myself!*

Her emotions overrode any fear she might have had. "Tomorrow!"

# CHAPTER 43

Using contacts she'd made working for Maggie, Claire found Sam Salvatore's office. Taking great care in 'dressing the part,' she set out on her mission.

No more running! Max had been right. It was time to stop running. She was going to meet her father and get the truth about her origin.

She was met by big bruisers. They had to be his security staff, or maybe just his bodyguards. They made it clear that no one just drops in to see Sam Salvatore.

"Then how do I meet him?" she confidently asked.

The one who seemed in charge turned and walked away to use his Bluetooth. "Hey Boss, there's a dame here who wants to see you." A pause. "Yeah, she's a real looker, Boss."

He disconnected and turned back to Claire, waving her toward him. "Hold on. I have to pat you down before you—"

"Is that really necessary?" she objected. Without a word, he quickly did the job and then indicated which elevator to take.

"Press the penthouse button. When you get out, you'll be at his place."

As the door closed, and the car started to rise, she muttered to herself, "First hurdle: done."

The door opened onto a modern, luxurious apartment. All glass walls allowed for panoramic views of the city. The heavy oak furnishings throughout the room, along with deep green overstuffed chairs and couch, seemed all wrong for the room. The inhabitant behind the over-sized, ornate desk appeared garish in his shiny blue suit.

Sam was pouring himself a cup of coffee (lots of cream and sugar, she noticed.) She walked into the room and waited for him to acknowledge her.

Finishing his chore, he turned toward her, then sat down. "Turn around," he said.

"I beg your pardon?" Claire asked.

"Just do it," Sam ordered.

Not knowing what else to do, she twirled. "Will that do?"

Sam took in her classy look: her figure, enhanced by the well-cut navy suit, which emphasized her deep-sea-blue eyes. She needed minimal makeup, and her blond highlights framed a beautiful face. And along with all that, she had spunk.

"OK, you might do."

"Might do what?" Claire quipped. She moved a chair nearer to him. "May I?" she asked.

As he had been looking her over, he got how she studied him. What was her angle? Maybe she was admiring his olive skin, black wavy hair, and bold, dark brown eyes. He worked at looking good. It was obvious that he worked out and paid big bucks for his custom-made suits. He wondered why she wasn't intimidated by him—but she wasn't.

Without waiting for permission, she sat. "Mr. Salvatore, I need some answers that only you can answer."

"Who the hell do you think you are talking to? Waltzing in here without an invitation? Do you want the job or not?" Sam put down his coffee and started to stand.

Claire blurted, "I'm your daughter!"

Sam sat back down and just glared at her. Then he began to laugh, a big, bellowing laugh. "Oh, that's rich, sister! That's a good one." His laughter stopped. "You think you are the first one to try that scam? You can leave! Don't ever come near my place again—and be grateful you are leaving with just a warning!"

Claire remained very still, calm. "I don't want your money or a job; I only want answers."

He shook his head, "Answers!" he said, then curious, "Is that right? All right. We will play your little game—ask away."

"My mother was Ruthie Malone. Does that ring any bells?"

Sam stiffened. "I don't know any Ruth Mallory," he growled.

"Malone—as in Casey Malone, his sister. And no, you wouldn't know her now—she is dead."

"Who are you?" Sam rose and stood in front of her.

"I told you. She was my mother, and you are my father."

He moved away from her. "What do you want?"

He was seething inside. Could she really be his daughter? Ruthie's daughter? Could that bastard, Casey, really have hidden her all these years?

"All I want to know is what really happened?"

"What are you talking about? What really happened when?" He looked puzzled, off balance, confused.

"Between you and my mother," Claire spoke more softly.

Sam got it. She wanted to hear a love story. Well, she wasn't going to hear one from him!

Sam straightened up. "Maybe I knew her, hard to know. Women couldn't keep their hands off me," he smirked. "So, if you're here to try to make something special out of a one-night stand, believe me: you aren't the first. You've come to the wrong address."

Claire looked appalled at this declaration.

Sam picked up his cup and took a sip of his now-cold coffee and put it down again.

"Look, kid. I'm sorry to put the kibosh on your story, but it just never happened."

"What never happened? You never raped her?" she shouted at him.

"Get out. Now! Out!"

Claire stood, shaking with fury, and left. She barely kept herself from running to the automated elevator, which opened as she approached. Once inside, she leaned against the wall for support. As soon as she was out of the building, she looked for a cab—to get her as far away from this place as possible.

Sam was furious—at Casey, at this woman who dared to confront him with such lies! No one talked to him that way, and they didn't last long if they tried. *Did Casey send her here? Is this his retaliation? Accusing him of rape!*

He paced the room, so agitated he couldn't stay in one place. *His daughter? Well, she sure had guts! That could have come from him—but she sure was no Italian—in fact, she looked so much like Ruthie...*

He stopped pacing. Memories—how much he loved Ruthie, their sweet times together—until Casey got in the way; separated them and then hid her! Of course, he had to go after her—make her remember how good they were together. Yeah, he pressed her—but women always say no when they mean yes.

He sat down at his antique-looking desk. No point rehashing all that. The girl? The woman? Ridiculous! Couldn't be his daughter. A son? Now, that might have been different. He smiled briefly. His hands had finally stopped shaking, and he took up the work on his desk.

# CHAPTER 44

Claire was caught between rage and frustrated tears. She directed the cab driver to her apartment. She hurried up the steps of the brownstone and pounded the elevator button for her floor.

In her modest apartment she had decorated with brightly colored fabrics on the floor and sofa, she threw off her heels and discarded her suit. After wrapping her comfy, terry-cloth robe around her, she headed for the kitchen, pulled a wine glass from the cupboard, and found the half-filled bottle of Maggie's gift. She poured the wine into her glass, feeling miserable.

Curling up in the corner of her sofa, she remembered how awful she had behaved to Casey and Max. They had tried to warn her. She gulped her wine. *Even Maggie.*

She cringed, remembering how awful she had been to her one true friend in this hard city.

Tears finally came, and she let them drip as she finished the wine. She wrapped a comforter around her. *And Max!* She couldn't afford to think about him right now. *He was so—what? All he wanted to do was protect her. She didn't need protection!* Somehow, though, she wished he had. And with that thought, she drifted into a troubled sleep.

The piercingly loud front door buzzer startled her awake. *What was that awful sound? Oh, the door.* "Who?" she called down.

"It's me, Claire. Max. Please let me in." She wasn't sure that was a good idea, but she buzzed the downstairs door and then ran to the bathroom. She hurriedly splashed cold water on her face, a quick swipe with the toothbrush, and a dash of lip gloss.

When she heard the knock on her door, she took a deep breath and let him in.

"You're OK?" Max asked.

"Of course I am; why wouldn't I be?" Claire said, hating the slight quiver in her voice.

He was uncertain how to respond, so he just walked in and gestured whether he should sit.

She felt awkward and somehow vulnerable, just standing as he sat. She asked if he'd like anything to drink before she caught sight of the empty wine bottle on the coffee table with her glass. "I haven't had a chance to clear things from last night," she apologized, and quickly took the two items into the kitchen. "You want coffee?"

"No, I'm fine. Thanks," he said, ignoring her discomfort.

"So, have you and Casey decided what's next for me?" she asked.

"Claire, I came because I had to know you were all right. Look, I've just talked with Dillon; I told him about our 'discussion' with Casey—"

"Oh, great! Another male added to the mix!"

"Come on, Claire. That's not it at all. We care about you! Why should that make you so angry? And if you *do* go see Sam, who knows what—"

"I DID go see Sam Salvatore," she said, trying to sound bold, but she instead dissolved into tears.

Max stood and gently pulled her into his arms. She didn't even try to resist.

"What happened?"

"He... he laughed at me!" Claire sobbed. Hurt pride, embarrassment, and anger vying for each other.

"Oh, Max! It was so awful. He rejected even the idea that I could be his daughter. He thought I was trying to con him! For money!" Her outrage took over. "He is a horrible man—disgusting—and he's my *father*!"

Claire almost collapsed as she said 'father.' Max held fast to her and then sat with her on the sofa. He let her cry, his arms around her.

At last, the sobs diminished and finally stopped. "I know you—and Casey—tried to warn me. I feel really dumb!" she said with a trace of a smile.

Max just gave her a hug. "How could you know? You were very brave, facing him like that. Dumb? Maybe, but also brave. He won't be able to haunt you anymore."

"Haunt?" She sniffed. "How do you mean?"

"I think you were searching for the ghost of a father you never knew. Your absolute determination to find him and face him wouldn't let you go. He was a powerful force in your life. Now, you *can* let him go."

"I wish I were so certain. Max, you should have

seen his face! He was furious when I accused him of raping my mother."

"You really did let him have it!" he said, surprised and disturbed.

"He may really want me dead after today!" Claire joked.

"Casey may have a good plan. I certainly hope so!"

# CHAPTER 45

Maggie knocked lightly and entered Casey's office. When she caught his attention, she said, "I've news—about Bobby."

He sat up with anticipation. "And?"

"I've kept my watchers alerted for any news about Bobby, whether alive or dead."

"Well?"

"He's in a jail in Guadalupe, Mexico, on some drug charges, I presume."

"Excellent! Get Dillon in here. This will fit into my plan nicely," He waved her out.

"Dillon, I have a task for you. You do have a passport, yes? And all your lawyer papers?"

"Sure. Of course."

"I want you to go down to Guadalupe, Mexico,

and get Bobby—you know, that kid who dated Claire—get him out of jail. Bring him directly to me. Tell him all is forgiven, and I have a job for him."

"OK," said Dillon hesitantly, not sure if he should quiz Casey for more details.

"Maggie will fill you in and arrange the contacts you will use down there."

Dillon stood there, still uncertain.

"*Now*, Dillon—please. This can't wait."

After Maggie and Dillon left, Casey took a phone out of his locked drawer and punched the keys. "It's me. I know. It's been awhile. But if I remember correctly, I owe you a favor." He laughed. "Yes, indeed, that is a switch, especially since this will be a doozie." He listened and then interrupted, "Sam Salvatore. You've wanted him for a long time, yes? Yeah, I know.... real evidence, and to get that, you need to provide a small favor." He listened again. "When I'm ready, you will be the first to know." He hung up, satisfied with how his plan was unfolding.

# CHAPTER 46

Bobby was still hungover when Dillon sat down in the dilapidated visitor's room to talk to him. Dillon couldn't tell whether the putrid smell was coming from Bobby or off the walls of the Mexican jail.

"Please," Dillon demanded, "Try to pay attention —closely." He waited for Bobby to finally look up. "I'm assuming you would like to get out of here," he said to the demoralized Bobby.

"Sure—I guess."

"To do that, you have to follow my instructions exactly."

Bobby sneered suspiciously, "What instructions?"

Concerned about being overheard, Dillon said cryptically, "Never mind, just do what I tell you."

Bobby was becoming more alert and argued, "Look, Man! I don't know you or what you want. Maybe I'm safer right where I am."

"Safer?" Dillon cocked one eyebrow. "I can do 'safer'—guaranteed. Can you?"

Bobby's sneer disappeared. He gulped. "So, what do I have to do?"

"Just keep your mouth shut, because we are leaving. Right now."

# CHAPTER 47

Casey welcomed Dillon back. Bobby had been dropped off with a couple of watchers assigned to get him cleaned up and unhungover.

"You got what you needed from my contacts down there?" Casey asked.

"Essentially, the money took care of everything, especially the bribes. No problem."

"Good, good." Casey drummed his fingers on his desk. "Tell me about Max."

Dillon was thrown by the question. "Max is a very good guy."

"Yeah. I expect you to say that. Not what I want to know."

Puzzled, Dillon asked, "What exactly...?"

Gruffly, he asked, "Is he good enough for Claire? Will she get hurt?"

"Oh." He took his time. "Well, she's a real firecracker." He cleared his throat. "He is the one more likely to get burned. He is so crazy about her. I worry she will hurt him."

Casey gave his characteristic *huh*. Then switching the subject once more, "OK Dillon. Keep me informed about Bobby. Let me know when he is ready to cooperate."

"Right," said Dillon, as he rose, glad to leave.

# CHAPTER 48

Maggie glanced at the elevator door as it opened and immediately stood up as Claire approached. Trying to sound upbeat, she said, "You can't see him right now." Her body blocked the door.

"Just for a few minutes," Claire said as she tried to go around Maggie.

Maggie was firm, "No, Claire. Come on, let's go get some coffee from the Cafe. I can use a break." She tried to urge her toward the elevator.

"Maggie, I'm sorry about how our dinner ended —"

"No worries—"

"But, it's important that I see Casey." Once again, she turned toward his door.

"Claire! No! He has someone with him, and he absolutely cannot be disturbed." Maggie softened as she said, "Claire, I have to ask you to leave."

"Maggie!"

"I promise to call you when he is free. Please, honey, it will all be OK soon."

"What will be OK?" Claire had never heard such urgency from Maggie in all the time she had been here. She took a deep breath. "All right. But just as soon as he is free." She slowly made her way to her office down the hall, wondering, *who in the world could he be talking to?*

# CHAPTER 49

As Bobby left Casey's office, he almost collided with Max, who was exiting the elevator.

Max let out, "Whoa! *You!*"

Bobby quickly got in the still-open elevator without saying a word.

Max faced Maggie. "What in the hell? How did *he* get in here? Was he with Casey? What's going on, Maggie?"

"Yes, he was found, as you saw. He's part of Casey's plan." She held up her hand, palm facing Max. "No, I don't know more than that."

"Well, when *will* we know?"

Maggie tried to dismiss him. "Casey will want to see you, but not right now, OK?"

"Is he in there, Maggie? I intend to get—"

Casey's voice rang out, startling them both:

"Maggie!"

She rolled her eyes. "Coming!" she responded. "Max, I will tell him you were here and need to see him." With that, she left him standing, frustrated and angry.

*Casey must have set something in motion with Bobby!* Max thought. *He knows Sam ordered the hit, and still, he said nothing to the rest of us!* He headed for the stairs, too aggravated to wait for the elevator.

Max fumed. Once in the lobby, he changed his mind. He turned around, took the next elevator back up, and strode toward Casey's office. He wasn't about to be dismissed like an errand boy!

*No Maggie at her post. Good!* He walked into the office without announcing himself, interrupting Casey dictating to Maggie.

"Come in, come in, Max," Casey called out, "That's good for now, Maggie."

She rose quickly and scurried past Max.

Surprised and a little apprehensive, Max hesitated before walking toward Casey.

"Sit, sit," said Casey. "I gave Bobby his marching orders. Now we just have to wait, and I hope not for long."

Max looked at Casey quizzically as he took a chair. "I thought we were going to do this together."

"Nah, nah—couldn't wait. I want it done now my way. Dillon was a great help. He got Bobby up here and, well, he has his orders, too."

Before Max reacted, Casey abruptly changed the subject. "Max, I'd like to have you on my team." At Max's look, he continued, "You know, come work for me."

Max was shocked into a spontaneous: "Doing what?!"

Casey smiled, settling more into his chair. "With whatever I want," then he amended, "whatever I need done."

"I don't think so." However, looking at Casey's expression, he added, "I told you before, I am only helping with Claire. Now that I have my law degree, I've decided it's best to be on my own and just take on cases where I can be most effective."

"Huh," Casey responded. Then he offered, "How about being my consultant?"

Max considered Casey's offer. He decided it would be wise to compromise. "As long as I would be free to accept or not accept any project offered,

I would consider working as a private contractor."

"That would work," Casey said, then went on, "as long as we both understand the need for loyalty."

"If, by that, you mean confidentiality, of course. That goes without saying."

Staring at Max fiercely, Casey said, "I need it clearly said!"

Max remembered Casey's seeming paranoia before offering, "I would always work under my license *as an attorney*."

The tension between them abated, and Casey said, "OK then! Settled. Maggie will get the non-disclosure paperwork to reflect that." Casey then surprised Max once again: He stood and offered his hand.

Max took it.

When Max had closed the door behind him, Casey sat back and chuckled to himself. *I like that guy! He's got grit. He'll do nicely for Claire.*

# CHAPTER 50

When Max left, Maggie buzzed Claire, "This might be a good time."

Claire hurried from her office, but before entering, she asked, "How is he?"

"OK." Maggie buzzed Casey, "Claire wants to see you."

"Sure, sure. Have her come in."

"Go on in." Maggie gave her an encouraging smile.

A little tentatively, Claire went in. Casey waved her to a chair, then limped around his desk to sit by her.

"So, what—" he began as she started speaking, "Casey, I am—"

They both stopped.

She started again, "Casey, I am so very sorry."

Tears threatened as she said, "I should have listened to you."

"What have you done?" he asked.

"I went to see Sam."

"I see. Huh! Then it looks like we'd better move fast."

Puzzled, she asked, "What do you mean?"

"Never you mind. I'm taking care of that." He turned to her. "What exactly did you tell him?"

"I told him I was his daughter... He laughed at me! He thought I was there for some kind of sleazy job. And then he accused me of trying a scam." Tears ran down her cheeks.

"When I accused him of raping my mother, he made it seem like she was nothing to him." Just remembering was so painful. "He threw me out of his office!"

Casey said nothing. He just studied her before he suggested, "That Max fellow might be very good for you."

"*What*?!" her voice close to a screech.

"He seems reliable. I think he would take good care of you."

Furious, she stood.

"*TAKE CARE OF ME? I'LL TAKE CARE OF ME,*

*thank you very much!"*

She left as fast as her heels allowed.

Casey watched her leave, a slight smirk on his face. *"Yep, just as Dillon said, a real firecracker."*

Claire couldn't believe that Casey would dare—well, there wasn't much Casey wouldn't dare. *Besides,* she considered as she walked slowly to her office, *Max has probably had enough of me by now.* He wasn't fond of her temper, which just seemed to erupt before she could stop it.

# CHAPTER 51

Sam tried to dismiss his confrontation with that woman who claimed to be his daughter. But it wasn't working. What would possess her to try such a scam?

Ruthie. Constant thoughts of Ruthie kept intruding. He was too distracted to work. *Casey! Was that Claire? Casey's protege?* It all started to make sense, bit by bit. But what did she want from me? He couldn't figure out that part.

She accused him of rape! That *had* to come from Casey! But how had—from Ruthie? Could this woman really be...?

He thought he had taken care of this Claire person, TWICE! Strange. Missed twice. Bobby had never let him down before. Where was that character anyway?

"Kurt!" The door opened.

"Yes, Boss?"

"Find Bobby—I want to talk to him—like Now!"

"Right, Boss!" Kurt exited fast.

* * *

"Hey! Bobby! Been lookin' for ya." Sam puffed on his Havana cigar. "For a while now."

Sam's greeting made Bobby even more nervous than when his man Kurt dragged him here.

"Hi, boss." Bobby couldn't quite stop the shakes inside.

"Where ya been, Boy?" Sam nodded for Kurt to take off.

"I just needed to take a break—you know."

"Sure. I just wished you'd told one of the boys—or me."

Bobby plunged in, "Really sorry, boss, but I'm ready to go! What's the job?" He'd soon know whether this was Casey's plan.

"Oh—the job." Sam plucked his cigar from the ashtray on his desk. He re-lit it until the tip glowed. "You know Mendez—from the cartel down at the docks?"

"Sure, we did a job together awhile back."

"I want you to set up a delivery to his chief," Sam said.

Bobby couldn't stop cracking his knuckles. *This was it! The plan might work!*

Sam instructed, "I'll get it ready. You set up the spot and the time with Mendez for the exchange. Use Raul and Freddy for your back up." Sam's voice stopped him from leaving, "Bobby! You tell no one else, got it?"

"Sure! How soon?"

Sam's dark eyes gleamed. "You'll tell me. I'm ready now. I've been waiting for you—capice?"

Bobby left—scared. This deal was exactly what Casey wanted. But Sam had never treated him quite like that before. What if he suspected? Anxiety bit into his gut.

*What if this was payback—for missing the shot with Claire? Was he being set up?*

He took the stairs down and headed for his apartment. *Some apartment! His room!* He hoped that was about to change.

As Bobby walked, he kept thinking about Casey's directions and the money promised. Set Sam up for a fall! Yeah! This was his golden opportunity to be free of Sam—he hoped. And earn Casey's trust.

He straightened up and walked more briskly. He knew Casey would want a report, but he figured Sam might have him followed. Casey could wait.

\* \* \*

Bobby was right. He was being watched—by Casey. When his men reported to their boss, Casey put the next part of his plan in motion.

He called his contact and let him know the bug on Bobby's phone was working fine. They would know the where and when the deal would go down as soon as Bobby set it up.

Casey left it to the FBI on how they wanted to get the drug war going. The cartel just had to believe Sam had double-crossed them. Casey had to wait for it all to unfold. Hopefully, Bobby would be taken care of at the same time.

# CHAPTER 52

Dillon was locking the door to his office when he heard footsteps on the stairs. He turned around and saw Max coming up. Delighted to see his long-time friend, he exclaimed, "Well, hello there!"

"You are just leaving?"

"Yeah—*Leaving* leaving," he said, pointing to the 'For Lease' sign on the door. "I was just taking a final look around, making sure the movers had taken everything."

Jokingly, Max asked, "So, are you taking that forest ranger job you were always talking about?"

"Not exactly." He paused. "Come on. Let's go get a drink." As the two started down the stairs, he said, "I'll fill you in on the latest."

After they had been served a couple of beers, Max nudged Dillon, "So, let's have it. What's going on?"

"You know, working for Casey. That really got me out of a difficult financial bind."

Poking fun at his friend, "Is that why you are moving your office—to what? more exclusive digs to better represent a successful lawyer?"

"Attorney—please!" he laughed, trying to accept the joke.

Dillon took a long pull at his beer before saying more. Then he blurted, "I've met someone." He paused when he saw Max's quizzical smile and the shake of his head. "No, Max. Not like that. This is different."

"Sorry, Buddy," he said, still smiling as he looked at Dillon. "But haven't we sung that song before?"

"I know, I know," Dillon acknowledged. "But this is for real, Max."

"OK. So who is she?" Max asked, trying to withhold his skepticism.

"Well, to begin with, I am sure I have a better chance with her as a successful attorney than as a forest ranger."

Dillon meant it to sound like a joke, but to Max, it was clear he meant it. He was serious.

Max was becoming a little more concerned for his friend, and responded, "Must be a bit of a whirlwind romance."

Dillon took a couple more swallows before continuing, "She is way out of my league, Max. I met her at one of Casey's meet-and-greet functions. She is stunning!" he effused. "Uniquely beautiful—and intelligent!"

Max, gently this time, teased, "Well, that alone has to set her apart."

"No, Max. I mean really smart! She heads up a real estate conglomerate—she's a key player in Casey's world. And the amazing part? She accepted a date with me! We've been seeing each other every day since."

Trying to match Dillon's enthusiasm, he asked, "For how long?"

"A month," Dillon replied, "And yeah, that's one reason to shut down the old office, which I wasn't hardly using, anyway."

Max hadn't seen Dillon so besotted in a very long time. He didn't know what to say as he watched Dillon finish his beer and then place bills on the table.

As Dillon was about to leave, Max stopped him, "Hang on! Look, I'm happy for you; I really am." Max was relieved when Dillon sat back down.

The skeptical look was gone, and Max's sincere tone encouraged Dillon to confess more.

"Casey sees what's happening between Sasha and me, and he's encouraging it! He has persuaded me to set up my office full-time in his building— No, I'm not an employee!" he exclaimed at the worried look on Max's face. Somewhat begrudgingly, he said, "I'm associated."

"That's great, Dillon. I wish nothing for you but happiness and good fortune." Max put his hand on Dillon's shoulder; gave it a quick squeeze.

Somewhat embarrassed, Dillon began moving again, "Look, Max, I've really got to run. Sasha does not tolerate tardiness," he said, smiling. "It's wonderful to see you again—let's do this more often." They shook hands, and Dillon departed.

Max sat again, somewhat dumbfounded as he watched his friend hurry away.

He truly hoped Dillon would find happiness in his life, but he had seen Dillon jump headfirst into entanglements before. In most of those encounters, if Max hadn't been there, Dillon would have been badly hurt.

He raised the bottle and was about to drink when the realization struck him: their relationship based on Max as his rescuer, was over. Dillon now would—or would not—grow up. Max finally admitted to himself that it was good that they both had let go. They each had to be responsible for their own lives.

As he finished his beer, it occurred to him that Dillon hadn't even asked about Claire. *Interesting,* he thought, and Max hadn't offered to tell him.

# CHAPTER 53

Bobby got on his assignment right away. How fast the plan became action depended on the availability of the drugs and the cartel's ability to get them into the U.S. by boat.

He put through the call to Mendez as he had been directed by Sam.

An automated response guaranteed the person he wanted would return his call within 48 hours. He had plenty to take care of while he waited for Mendez.

Raul and Freddie were set to ride shotgun. Sam provided the steel briefcase of $100,000. The warehouse used for their usual drops would do.

Bobby was glad that it was Mendez he would meet. He was unlike most of the guys in the cartel, who were a little scary with their guns always at the ready. Nobody would even think about pulling a fast one with those guys. Not even Sam... or Casey.

Waiting around for Mendez to get back to him with confirmation of date and time was a drag. Too much time to worry. Casey would check every move he made—and if this didn't go down as Casey planned, it would be Sam who'd take care of Bobby!

Everything came together more smoothly than Bobby could have expected. A drug shipment had already been underway with its load of cocaine, fentanyl, and heroin. Within five days, everything was in place. This was his first run, and the adrenaline was flowing as he drove the van with the two muscle guys Sam had provided for security.

The streets were deserted at two in the morning, the time agreed upon for the meet. Bobby nervously kept mouthing the combination for the locks on the steel briefcase containing the money. He didn't dare write anything down. The two in the back seat had their assault rifles armed and ready.

"Here we go!" Bobby said as he approached the

wide doors.

One of his guys jumped out of the van to give the signal to open up. The garage-like door rose noiselessly.

Bobby drove in, making a large circle in order to back in toward the center.

The large warehouse was empty and barely lit, except in the center where the trucks were to park and make the exchange. So far, they were the only ones there. Bobby's stomach was roiling. Cracking his knuckles as they waited wasn't helping.

A few minutes later, the truck from the cartel came toward the van from the opposite entrance and made the same circular approach, so the rear end would be opposite that of the van.

Each driver signaled, flashing their headlights twice, indicating the occupants should exit their vehicles; guns drawn were expected from both sides.

Mendez stepped down out of his vehicle and opened the rear doors of his truck. He turned and facing the van, signaled for Bobby to get out, and come forward with the money.

Bobby clutched the briefcase to him as he exited. Raul and Freddy were close behind, one on each side of him.

Bobby's adrenaline spiked. Things felt wrong. *It wasn't supposed to happen this way! Shouldn't I make sure of the product before handing over the money?*

Bobby was flooded with uncertainty. He watched Mendez, who had both arms extended slightly away from his sides, waiting.

What exactly was Mendez doing?

The gesture...

Suddenly, shots rang out.

Two cartel guys alongside Mendez revealed their assault rifles. They shot at Bobby and his back-up men.

Bobby went down first. Freddy died next. Raul was unconscious.

Mendez ran to Bobby, made sure he was dead, then grabbed the briefcase and signaled his men to get back in the truck. He jumped behind the wheel and roared off in the same direction they had come in from. The truck's tires screeched on the concrete floor.

As they neared the exit, congratulating each other about how easy it had all gone down, they were greeted with a hail of bullets that exploded through the windshield, killing Mendez. The truck slowed to a stop and was quickly surrounded.

A bullhorn bellowed: "FBI! Throw down your guns; put your hands behind your head; exit the vehicle!"

Two men, one dead, the other wounded, were pulled out of the truck and placed beside the body of Mendez. The remaining cartel boys were quickly handcuffed and loaded into an FBI van.

Product from the cartel and the money in the briefcase were confiscated and transferred to the agents' vehicle. A waiting ambulance and the Medical Examiner's van drove into the warehouse. Attendants took care of the unconscious Raul. All the bodies were sent to the morgue to await the ME.

Captain Ramos from the FBI congratulated his people for a perfect takedown. That 'anonymous' tip had really paid off.

As Captain Ramos was driven off, he made a call from the car.

"It went down just as you said. Yeah, like clockwork." Ramos listened, then said, "I guess we owe *you* one now. (He heard Casey chuckle). Thanks for helping get these scum off the earth," he said. "Oh, one of the cartel guys was wounded, but he should recover—at least enough to give us lots of information. And one of Sam's men, a Raul, might regain consciousness. He looked like he was dead, but he's holding on so far. That would be a coup! So, thanks again."

Casey put his phone down, leaned back in his chair, and congratulated himself on a good night's work.

Just before dawn, Casey's people awakened him with more news of the previous night. As he drank his first cup of coffee, they told him that Sam was on the run.

Casey knew nothing was finished until Sam was contained. No one was going after him yet. But the cartel had been disrupted, and they, hopefully, would take care of Sam. In any case, The FBI would get a warrant for his arrest soon.

Casey poured another cup of coffee. He was happy that Bobby had been taken down. The mole was gone.

The real war now was between the two corrupt forces: Sam's people and the Cartel, all while the

Feds watched. That would eliminate future difficulties for him.

Yes, Casey could afford a smile.

* * *

Sam was livid as word quickly reached him. It was a disaster! How could Bobby or Mendez have botched his plan so thoroughly? He admonished himself: *Forget it. Just get going!*

He went into action mode: gave instructions to his key people, grabbed the go-bag he always had ready, and headed to his Mercedes and took off. He wasn't about the wait for a confrontation with the cartel or the Feds on his doorstep.

He had to prepare for war!

* * *

Casey told Maggie to bring Claire to his office right away. He wasn't about to take chances with her life while Sam was still on the loose. He had to be sure that the rest of his plan played out. Hopefully, it would be over soon, but he couldn't count on it.

When Claire arrived, he gave her one of his rare smiles, which immediately put her on alert.

"Time for a vacation, don't you think?"

Her astonished "What?" was cut off by his coming around his desk with an envelope in his hand. "This will give you lots of time to relax." At her bewildered look, he added, waving the envelope, "Enough here to make a fine shopping trip! But probably best to do that when you get there." As he shoved the thick envelope into her hands, he turned her toward the door and walked her out. "No thanks needed—you've earned it."

Why did he sound so jovial? This was just too bizarre.

"Make up for all our lost time as a family!" he said, and she was out the door that he shut firmly behind her.

# CHAPTER 54

Claire left the office and was entering the elevator as Max was ushered into Casey's office. Casey welcomed him with a hearty clap on the back and surprised Max with, "Max, Max, come on in!"

He shrugged off the effusive welcome and asked, "What progress, Casey?"

"It's almost finished." And then he amended, "Except for Sam as yet." He then disclosed all that had gone down so far. He explained his plan to get Claire out of the way, temporarily. He needed Max to be sure it would happen.

"Here are the means," Casey said. "You take my jet; you tell the pilot where to go. Here is the money to keep you both busy for as long as it takes to make sure Sam is out of the picture."

Max demanded before accepting the thick envelope, "No more danger for Claire?"

"It's up to you to make sure that she's out of harm's way until there's no more Sam."

Max assured him that would happen.

"One final instruction," Casey said, "No one is to know where you are—except Maggie. She will give you a special number to call. When you arrive at your destination, you call that number. No one will contact you until it's safe to come back. Be sure Maggie gives you the code that will identify her—and no one else. If you hear any other voice, even with the code, you get Claire away from there fast."

Max nodded his understanding and agreement. Casey extended his hand, which after a moment's hesitation, Max accepted. Both realized how dangerous the situation remained until Sam was dealt with, finally.

# CHAPTER 55

Claire was befuddled, a silly word, but she couldn't come up with a more accurate description of how she felt. She hailed a cab to take her home.

Vacation? At least she was no longer questioning how Casey felt about her—just wondering if maybe he had lost his mind!

Once home, she brewed a cup of tea. It brought back sweet memories of a tiny lady in a tiny tea shop—with Max. She sighed, sipped her tea, and decided to see what exactly was in the packet Casey had given her.

She gasped at what she found: a new passport— for a Connie Massey; one Visa card, one American Express card, and various membership cards in that same name. And a whole lot of money, which she was too shocked to count. She just sat and stared at all of it. *What in the world?*

Her reverie broke at the insistent sound of the doorbell. *Now what*?! she wondered. She pressed the intercom button and called down, "Yes?"

"It's Max."

Claire buzzed him into the building. At her door stood Max, holding a beautiful bouquet of the special lilies she had seen in his magical garden. She stepped aside to let him in.

He went directly to the kitchen and began opening cupboards, looking for a vase.

"I don't have any vases."

"Then we'll improvise," he said as he pulled down a tall glass pitcher. He filled it with water and arranged the flowers. "Where shall we put them?" he asked.

"Max. Stop! What is going on?"

He set the pitcher on the dining table, "You don't like them?"

"I *love* them; how did you know...?" She stopped. And for a moment, she pictured Max's beautiful garden with the breathtaking lilies—and her comment. *He had heard and remembered!*

Claire turned to him. "They are truly lovely," she said as she gazed into his eyes.

She then took a breath to say, "I don't know what is going on. First, Casey tells me to go on vacation, then gives me false identity papers. You show up, bringing my very favorite flowers, which makes no sense at all, and now you are all bubbly as if everything is just peachy keen!"

Max smiled at her, "I know." He put his hands on her shoulders and then a hand under her chin to be sure she was looking once again into his eyes. "I know," he said gently.

"Casey did a fast one on me too. Look!" He pulled out the envelope Casey had given him. "Two tickets to Barbados (which we aren't supposed to use.) Here is a letter, instructing the pilot of his private jet to get his destination from the holder of this letter only after the plane is in the air and out of range of the control tower. And, by the way, file a false flight plan! Oh and here is the fun part: a boatload of money to provide for our needs until he orders us back."

"We?" Did she want that? The twinge of excitement in her belly was a clue.

"Yes. We. Casey is making sure you are out of harm's way, as he puts it, while the Sam issue is unclear."

"That Man!" she cried. "So manipulative. Tells me to leave. Orders who I go with. Explains nothing!" In a teasing tone, she added, "Maybe I don't want to go; or go with YOU! Nobody asked what I would like! I just—"

Max said nothing. He just pulled her to him and kissed her until she melted into his arms.

"Are you sure you don't want company?" he asked and then released her. "I mean, I have my orders to keep you safe, but I don't have to be *with* you. Hm—we could agree that I stay no closer than ten paces away from you at all times," he teased. "I don't want you to feel obligated in any way—"

"Oh, shut up!" she said, moving close to him again, about to kiss him.

"Are you sure this is what you want?" he asked, preventing the kiss.

"At this exact moment—Yes!"

He pulled her into his arms, but let her initiate the kiss.

Later, sitting close on the sofa, they were interrupted by his cell phone. Max listened carefully and acknowledged that he understood.

He kissed Claire once more, and then casually

mentioned that he had one more small assignment for Casey to take care of before they could leave.

Max hugged her to him as they discussed where to go? He came up with one idea and she another. They both wondered, where *should* they go?

He suggested that she get started packing, as he left to do Casey's bidding.

# CHAPTER 56

Maggie was on the alert for any word concerning Sam. She wasn't sure what Casey would do if his plan to let the Cartel take care of Sam didn't pan out.

Casey was outraged by the way Sam had treated Claire. He had held back from dealing with Sam for years. Maggie knew the complicated reasons: childhood friendship, Ruthie, now Claire, kept him avoiding the issue. But now Sam had gone too far, and nothing would hold Casey back. Hopefully, without getting his own hands dirty.

Maggie was rearranging Claire's interviews with prospective clients. Some she would take, others she could farm out to some newer recruits. She would be so glad when everything returned to normal—if it ever would.

She was so deep in thought she hadn't registered that Casey was standing beside her. "Oh, Casey! You startled me! I didn't hear you call."

He chuckled, "Maggie, my girl. I think we deserve a treat. Come on. We're going to lunch."

"Together?"

"Yes, together! What do you think?" he said as he took her coat from the hook and helped her into it.

"But what about Sam? How can we celebrate—"

"Enough now about that SOB!" Casey snapped. "So, what sounds good to you?" he resumed as they closed themselves into the elevator.

# CHAPTER 57

The Mercedes navigated the slick streets nicely. Sam was sure he could get out of the City without being detected. He would gather his team once he got over the Canadian border. He congratulated himself on always being prepared: provisions, money, documents—all hidden in the car, should he ever need to escape.

Nah, this wasn't escaping! This was being smart. Get out of town, make a plan, execute. The only real surprise was that he was driving north instead of to his estate in Manzanillo, Mexico.

Sam knew the Cartel would assume he was responsible for the double-cross. The only good part was knowing that Bobby was dead. He was sorry Mendez was taken out, but he was happy to be rid of Bobby.

The car slipped a bit. He slowed down slightly. The roads grew slicker as he got farther north.

He returned to his musings. *The big unanswered question was who tipped the Feds?* He had plenty of enemies. Someone was out to get him. Casey? *Nah...* he couldn't imagine Casey putting any plan together that would include the Feds! *Could he?*

Light beams from behind his car started to really annoy him. The idiot had his brights on. As much as he wanted to confront the guy, he admonished himself to play it smart and just slow down. Let the stupid jerk pass him.

But it didn't. It got closer and closer.

Hairs on the back of his neck prickled. He clutched the steering wheel more tightly. He tried to reassure himself: *they couldn't put someone on his tail that fast!*

The sudden bump on his car's back bumper shocked him. The second hit was unnerving.

Sam sped up; maybe he could outrun whoever was behind him.

The rear window shattered. *That's supposed to be bulletproof!*

*Damn, a little late to figure out you can't shoot*

*and drive! Or at least, he couldn't.*

It was harder and harder to hold the car on the icy road at the speed he was driving, but he was afraid to slow down. He was sweating now and wanted to turn down the heat. He didn't dare take a hand off the steering wheel. As the road climbed, full of twists and turns, Sam began to panic. He couldn't keep the car from swerving.

One final push from the attacking sedan at just the right moment, and Sam's Mercedes went over the edge, falling and bouncing until it landed and burst into flames.

After pulling their car over to the side of the road, the men got out of their sedan to make sure there wasn't a survivor.

# CHAPTER 58

Maggie was making the morning coffee in the alcove as Casey came in. "Did you run into traffic?" she asked.

"Why?"

"I can't remember when you were this late coming in." She brought his coffee, the usual cream and sugar, to him at his desk as he sat.

"How am I supposed to keep you on your toes if I don't change things around once in a while?" he said jovially, which earned him a skeptical look from Maggie.

"Nah. I just took my time and enjoyed my breakfast for a change." Casey gave Maggie a smile. "Anything I should be looking at right away?"

"Not really. Oh, you did get an anonymous

phone message. I saved the message for you. All the man on the phone said was, 'Thank you. We owe you one.'"

"I like that kind of message," he said as he picked up one of the reports she had put on his desk.

# CHAPTER 59

Maggie had the watchers she depended on for authentic information investigating the whereabouts of Sam. By now, she knew he had taken off in his Mercedes as soon as news of the FBI raid reached him. But before informing Casey, she wanted the particulars. Sam was a danger to all of them until he was contained.

She hadn't wanted to know how involved Casey had been in that whole takedown. And he hadn't shared any details with her. But with Sam still loose, she was determined to find out.

Claire almost ran out of the elevator, looking for her. "Maggie—what do you know? What's happening? Is Casey OK? Have you seen Max? We were supposed to leave an hour ago—"

Maggie stopped her in mid-stream to slow her

down, "Hey! Hey! Everything is OK. Casey is fine. I'm sure Max is too."

"Everyone is talking about an FBI raid. It's even on the news!" she exclaimed.

"I know... look, our people are investigating. We'll know all the facts soon." Maggie hoped fervently that what she was saying was true.

"Why aren't they telling us who got shot—or at least who survived?"

"The Feds never tell the public anything. You know that's how it is."

Maggie's reassurance calmed Claire somewhat. Maggie continued, "We'll know everything soon."

Still anxious, Claire asked, "What about Sam?"

"What about him?"

Becoming irritated, "Come on, Maggie. You know the whole point..."

"SH! Not out here, Claire!" Her voice a hoarse whisper.

Urgently whispering back, "You don't know?!"

Maggie shushed her again. "When I know you will know. I promise."

Casey interrupted their whispered exchange, saying as he came out of his office, "Ladies." He took in their worried expressions. "Much too nice a day for frowning."

Maggie spoke uneasily while trying to match his smile, "What do you need, Casey? Can I get you something?"

"No, no. I thought I heard Claire's voice out here. Come on in, Claire, come in."

Hoping to learn more than Maggie was willing to disclose, she acquiesced, following him into his room.

"I thought you might be a little worried about Max—" he began.

Startled, she asked, "Should I be?"

"No, no. That's my point." He huffed, then resumed, "He's on an assignment for me."

Pretty enigmatic, she thought. Probing, she asked, "I thought you sent him on a vacation."

"Yes, yes. I did. With YOU."

"Exactly!"

Casey practically sputtered, "So why are you here? Why aren't you home—packing? Waiting for Max?"

She looked for some sign or signal from him that she should keep pushing for answers. Sarcastically, she said, "He's on 'assignment' for you, right?"

He said nothing.

"Casey—"

"You need to be at home! Now. Right now."

"Will you please STOP!"

Casey was surprised into asking, "Stop what?"

"Ordering me to do this; don't do that! Trying to manipulate my life! Managing me! I don't care if you are my boss or my uncle. You can't—"

Frustrated with her, he blared, "I have to protect you! You are my Family!"

Shaking with fury, "Oh, PLEASE! Will the men in my life please. Stop. Protecting me!"

They stood glaring at each other. Casey then stepped over to her, putting his hands on her shoulders. He looked directly into her eyes, trying to make her understand. "But that's our job, Claire. That's what we do."

She took a shuddering breath. "Well, why don't you just—" and suddenly she blurted, "take care of Maggie?" Looking up, she saw the incomprehension on his face. "She adores you. She would love to have you 'protect' her." The last was said with implied meaning.

Casey moved back a step as he dropped her arms. "What are you talking about?"

*Why would she say such a thing? Where had*

*she gotten the idea that he and Maggie—*

Claire shook her head at his lack of understanding and gave up. No point in trying to get information. She left him puzzling over her words.

Casey stood woodenly, wondering at the possibility—him and Maggie?

Claire stopped at Maggie's desk on her way out. "Get ready, Maggie. I think things may be changing around here." She smiled at a confused Maggie and left for her office to continue waiting for news.

# CHAPTER 60

Things had changed. With Sam on the run, Casey had sent Max on a mission to discover Sam's escape destination.

Max was the only man he trusted with *this* job.

Claire and Max's 'vacation' had been put on hold.

Max, through his P.I. contacts, quickly got reports about a chase and a crash on the I-85 going north.

Taking his time on the icy roads, Max arrived at the crash site as the fire engine pulled away, and the ambulance was about to get underway. At about 100 feet away from the crash site, he parked off the road and got out of the car. He approached one of the policemen setting up crime tape around the affected area.

Very few of his questions were answered. Max did find out that there were no survivors, and no, they didn't know the identity of the one person in the vehicle; he should check with the coroner's office—no idea how long it would take. He also ascertained that the burned-out car was a Mercedes sedan. Same model as Sam's.

Shivering, Max hurried back to his car. Once it started, he turned around and drove back to the City. He was pretty certain that it was Sam—or what was left of him—in the ambulance. A call to the coroner would confirm it.

Once down and off the mountain roads, Max got on a toll road and drove into the next rest stop where he could pick up cell phone coverage.

After buying a large, black coffee, he called and reported to Casey, "I will know in a bit. But it looks like Sam's car crashed with Sam inside."

Casey told him, "Don't tell Claire until we are certain that Sam is dead."

Max thought Casey was much too paternalistic but agreed. He hoped that Claire would understand—eventually.

When would she accept that Casey—and he—cared about her? He and Casey both wanted definite proof that Sam could no longer hurt anyone. Even if in prison, Sam could cause damage.

Casey instructed Max to find out who had caused Sam's demise. Casey's FBI contact had assured him that faking the car accident wasn't them.

Could he be satisfied with just *believing* the Cartel had been responsible? He guessed that as long as no one came after him or Claire, he could live with it. He chuckled at his own pun.

# CHAPTER 61

Although Claire was relieved when Max came back to the apartment, she was not happy with his orders from Casey: 'Don't tell Claire until you hear from me.'

Upset, as well as anxious, she was furious at Max for letting Casey dictate what he could and could not tell her.

Fortunately, it was only two days later the ME's office reported that the body's DNA confirmed that the deceased was Sam Salvatore. Max now had Casey's 'blessing' to let Claire know, which defused her anger at Max.

Claire hardly knew how to react to the news that Sam was definitely gone—her father was gone. She was relieved, but also sad that the father she had always wanted to know turned out to be a horrible man who actually tried to kill her. Her uncle, Casey, had been a true father. She chuckled to herself at how she had been so mad at him for protecting her even when she strongly objected.

She looked up at Max. "He really, truly is dead?"

"Really, Truly," he assured her.

Claire took a deep breath. "I am so glad we are rid of that awful man!" she declared. "So, what do we do now?"

"Well, we still have *Uncle* Casey's gift, that is, if you still want to go," he teased.

"So when are we leaving? Do we still get to use the corporate jet? Did we actually decide where we are going?"

He cut the 'conversation' short by saying, "I'll talk to Casey about that. Just pack for warm beach weather."

Claire laughed as she watched him almost bouncing as he strode down the corridor. As she closed her door, she reminisced about all the changes in her life. Instead of running away as far as she could go, which turned out to be Costa Rica, she had faced her fears. No, she wasn't happy about her father. Certainly, he was not the father she had hoped to find. But she had stood up to him as well as to Casey and Max.

As Claire took down her suitcase from the shelf in the hall closet, she thought about the future. *Maybe a future with Max?* Beach weather, he had instructed. Sounded wonderful.

Within a day, they were boarding the jet Casey had authorized. She took in the smell of the luxurious leather seats. There was even a couch in the back.

The flight attendant took their orders for drinks. "Champagne, please," directed Max.

As they began to settle in, the hum of the jet engines increased her excitement.

Until they were in the air, Max didn't tell her that Casey assumed that this was their honeymoon.

"HONEYMOON!?" She almost dropped her glass. "Will he ever get the message that I am in charge of my life?" She stood up, facing Max to say, "Whether I get married—if ever—and to whom..."

She looked almost ready to run again—until Max pulled her onto his lap. With that last word on her lips, Max kissed her.

And then, holding her very close, he whispered in her ear, "Why don't we save the fireworks for later," and kissed her again before she could object.

*If you like this story,*
*would you be so kind as to leave a review?*

*Reviews are extremely important*
*to an author's success and greatly appreciated.*
*Even one sentence helps!*

To sign up for Mia's Newsletter,
visit MiaFliers.com.

An actress, a teacher, a financial planner, a commissioner, an executive assistant, a librarian—and now, Mia Fliers is an author, who put on paper a life, or lives of people who seek meaning, a purpose for being.

From her childhood Nancy Drew's adventures to the heroines she has portrayed as an actor, Mia Fliers spends her time diving into imaginary worlds. Without fail, she carries a paperback in her bag, whether working or heading to a Nichiren Buddhist meeting.

However, Mia never dreamed that she could write a novel.

A creative writing workshop taught by her friend and former student—awarding-winning playwright, Suzan Zeder—convinced Mia to give it a whirl. "Firecracker: Claire's Journey" is the result.

Mia fell in love with the process of writing. Her second novel, "The Shift: A Novel", is slated to be published in the Summer of 2020.